The Virgin Heart
Copyright©2016 Jimi Goninan
ISBN 978-1-909934-98-6
Cover art and design by Dawné Dominique

Published by
Lydian Press 2016
Find us on the World Wide Web at
www.lydianpress.com

THE VIRGIN HEART

Jimi Goninan

Lydian Press

For Chris

Thanks for all your encouragement and support
...and for being my favourite cheerleader.

THE VIRGIN HEART

Abraham Chadwick was most assuredly a virgin… much to his great chagrin. Despite being all of eighteen years of age, not a single part of him had been introduced to the pleasures of the flesh, barring the ministrations of his own hands, of course. His heart was also in a pristine state; never having been touched by the caress of romantic love. It wasn't that Abraham didn't know what he wanted, far from it. Outside the companionable bounds of friendship, Abraham hadn't had even the vaguest hint of attraction to womankind. For as long he could remember, Abraham had been drawn to the male of the species, from childhood crushes on teachers, to fellow students and even some of his neighbors – in particular, the handsome married gents, the Deacons, who lived directly behind his house and appeared to have little concern of being seen when they frolicked about in their backyard.

Nor was it due to a lack of physical appeal on Abraham's behalf. Indeed, his sparkling blue eyes, silky auburn hair and clear complexion made for a rather fetching combination. He'd even done a spot of sneaky surveillance in the locker rooms from time to time – as boys are wont to do – to ensure that he was definitely more than adequate when it came to the measure of his manhood. Years of competitive swimming had also honed his body into a lean and wonderfully defined specimen of fitness. Abraham loved to swim and being in the water had always felt as natural to him as walking on land. His parents had even had a heated pool installed, after he'd relentlessly campaigned for some years, so that he could swim in their backyard all year round.

His chaste status wasn't even due to a lack of opportunity, as there were quite a large number of eligible openly gay students at his high school, St. Francis Xavier. Originally, it had been an all-boys school staffed exclusively by priests, but it had converted to co-ed admissions about a decade previously and had consequently become far less strict in regards to its religious instruction. Discrimination of any kind was not tolerated and this more enlightened attitude had happily led to an open and safe atmosphere for all the students.

Rather, the main problem was that Abraham was painfully shy when it came to matters of the heart – and the crotch – and found it hard to talk to any guys he liked in a more than strictly platonic way. Even if he hadn't been so bashful, Abraham didn't wish to have sex with just anyone, as he wanted his first time to be with someone he loved – an old-fashioned notion perhaps, but one in which he truly believed. That being said, there were often times when his hormones got the better of him and his body cried out for the touch of any good-looking male who happened to be passing by.

Another impediment was that, outside of his small circle of close friends, Abraham wasn't particularly open about his sexuality – not even his family was privy to his predilections. His main sounding board for such concerns was his ever-loyal best friend, Topher, who lived right next door and had listened to Abraham's worries about his virgin condition with great patience over the past few years. Unlike Abraham, however, Topher was out and proud and even had a steady boyfriend, Eli. Abraham was awfully envious of Topher's confidence, and thriving sex life, to say the least.

It was coming to the end of the summer and Abraham was getting ready to start his senior year. In spite of the fact that Abraham sometimes felt he was little more than a complicated mess of rampaging hormones and heightened emotion, he hoped that this would be the year that things changed for him. His greatest desire, apart from getting into a good college, was to take that other next big step towards adulthood and finally get a boyfriend. Besides, his sexual energy really needed to go somewhere other than his hand, which frankly bordered on developing carpal tunnel syndrome from overuse.

Why can't I find a hot guy who will just sweep me off my feet and pound me senseless? Is it really too much to ask? At this rate, I'll be a virgin until I'm thirty!

* * *

It was almost the end of the first week of school and things seemed to be going as they always had for Abraham – classes, swim training and no miraculous arrival of the perfect match into his world. Granted, there seemed to be a heightened sense of camaraderie amongst the senior class, with people being even friendlier towards Abraham than normal. He just put the excess affability down to his classmates already beginning to feel nostalgic about their dwindling high school days and the big changes coming their way.

Behind Abraham, the wide hallway was bustling with the customary sounds of students making their way to class, banging locker doors and calling out to one another amongst the constant babble of conversations. Abraham was turning the combination to his locker when he felt the unexpected sensation of a strong, warm hand touch his upper arm.

"Pardon me," asked a deep, confident voice with a distinct southern drawl, from beside him. "Can ya help me?"

Abraham turned to see a boy around his age with caramel-colored skin, wide handsome features, framed by short, cropped, black hair.

He's gorgeous! Who is he?

"Y...yes." Abraham was so nervous he was surprised he hadn't lost the power of speech completely. "How can I help?"

"I'm Lincoln. I only just transferred here from New Orleans and I'm a bit lost. Can ya tell me where Mr. Peterson's English would be?"

"Oh, that's right beside my next class. It's not far." Abraham's heart fluttered wildly in his chest and he desperately hoped that he didn't look as flustered as he felt. "I can take you there if you like?"

"That'd be mighty kind of ya, thanks. What's your name?"

"Abraham."

"You're kidding, right?"

"Ah...no."

"Guess we were meant to find one another then," remarked Lincoln laughing.

"What?"

Lincoln gave a brilliant flash of white teeth in a smile that traveled all the way up to his kind brown eyes. Befuddled, Abraham found it exceedingly hard to concentrate.

"Our names…Abraham and Lincoln." Lincoln explained in an expectant tone.

"Oh, right."

Ergggh, why am I so dumb? He must think I'm a complete moron!

"Sorry, lame joke I know," said Lincoln, in a charming show of self-depreciation.

"No, it was funny…Guess I'm just a little slow today."

As they walked, Abraham sneaked several furtive glances at his new companion; very much appreciating the way Lincoln's electric-blue polo clung to his decidedly muscular torso. His eyes were also drawn to the extra-large red sneakers Lincoln was wearing.

If his feet are that big then maybe his…

Abraham pushed the thought aside before he became noticeably aroused – an embarrassingly easy occurrence of late given his unrequited yearnings. All too soon, for Abraham at least, they reached the door to the classroom.

"Well…this is it," said Abraham reluctantly.

"Thanks, I really appreciate your help. It's awful tough being new. See ya 'round, Beau."

Beau? Did he really call me, beautiful? Nobody calls me that…well except for mom but she doesn't really count. He was probably just making another joke I didn't get.

Lincoln flashed Abraham another warm, dazzlingly white smile before he turned and went into his class.

"Yeah…bye," mumbled Abraham.

Damn the back of him is just as hot as the front! I have no chance.

Abraham's face heated with an almost overpowering combination of embarrassment and arousal. In a bit of a daze, he slowly turned and made his way next door for his French class with Madame Perchet – a razor-thin, gray-haired harridan of a woman who seemed to take great delight in mercilessly chastising those who dared massacre her beloved language. She walked with an ivory-topped cane that she liked to brandish in the direction of unruly students and was generally feared amongst the student population…and by some of her colleagues, if truth be told.

The rest of the afternoon whisked past in a veritable blur for Abraham, and it would be safe to say that he absorbed absolutely nothing from his lessons. Every time he tried to focus on the class, Lincoln's smile would reappear and everything else simply faded away.

* * *

The following Monday, Abraham was sitting midway up the bleachers by the football field, eating his lunch with Topher – it was their habitual spot. They liked to eat there, as the view over the field and surrounding parkland was quite picturesque, especially when the football team was practicing, which they were currently doing, running up and down the field, their muscles straining against their snug uniforms. The shrill sound of the coach's whistle periodically punctured the air, as the pair talked and ate, while enjoying the warmth of the sunshine-filled day.

Abraham and Topher had been best friends ever since his next-door neighbors, the Walkers, had adopted Topher two years earlier. Topher hadn't had the happiest of adolescences to that point, having been thrown out of his home at the tender age of fifteen, after word of his assumed homosexuality had gotten back to his strictly religious and highly conservative family. When confronted by his parents about the rumors, Topher had courageously chosen to answer honestly and, after a great deal of yelling, they'd callously disowned him. Fleeing his small hometown of Magnolia Falls, Topher had ended up on the streets of Port Davinica, struggling to survive. In a happy turn of events, Topher had been rescued from a bleak-looking future when a man that he'd attempted to rob – driven purely by the need to eat – had taken pity on the unfortunate lad and helped set him on a better path. Instead of turning him over to police, the Good Samaritan had taken Topher into his home. The man in question, Lucien, happened to be the boyfriend of the Walker's biological son, Oliver, and after a brief period of fostering they had petitioned to adopt Topher. Since then, Topher hadn't had any meaningful contact with his biological parents. They hadn't even tried to contest the issue when Topher had been made a ward of the state, something Abraham found incredibly hard to fathom.

How could they abandon their own son? He's better off without them!

Abraham had been utterly horrified by his friend's story and it had made him appreciate his own liberal upbringing and supportive parents, even if he wasn't ready to come out to them just quite yet.

When they'd first met, Abraham had had quite the crush on Topher. This was unsurprising, given that Topher had alluring, liquid-brown eyes, adorably floppy dark-brown hair, honey-colored skin and a short but pleasing build. Naturally, given his shy nature, Abraham hadn't said a word about his attraction and by the time he was vaguely contemplating making a move, Topher was well and truly enamored with his current boyfriend, Eli. The couple had met when Topher had joined the school wrestling team, of which Eli was a star member.

Not that he begrudged them their happiness – too much. Of course, Abraham had been slightly disappointed but valued having Topher in his life, regardless. In fact, Abraham thought that Topher and Eli made a pretty good match in both personality and looks, as Eli's curious green eyes, vibrant red and black mess of curls atop his head and solid, pale frame contrasted beautifully with Topher's darker coloring. Besides he rather liked Eli, everyone did. In addition to his wrestling team glory, Eli played the part of the school mascot – Blaze the Bear – rather appropriate given his natural hairiness and was just one of those people who got along with absolutely everyone.

Topher was Abraham's most trusted confidante and vice versa. They discussed pretty much everything and consequently Abraham knew far more about Topher's sex life than Eli would've probably liked. Indeed, Topher was finishing up one such sordid story.

"I'd just sprayed all over his hairy little butt, when we heard the football team coming back in from practice. There wasn't even time to clean up! We only just got our pants back on before they came in," said Topher, laughing through his words.

"You're so lucky. You could've been caught!"

"Meh, it's not like they would've cared. I mean they always have a massive circle jerk together after practice."

"They do not!" protested Abraham, although the idea certainly had appeal.

"Well, I've never seen it personally but Eli assures me it's true."

"He'd know," quipped Abraham with just the slightest tinge of jealousy.

The subject of Eli's promiscuity before he'd met Topher had been well discussed by the friends.

"Hey! That's my one true love you're talking about!" exclaimed Topher, his face awash with mock outrage.

"I'm ever so sorry for daring to disparage the pristine virtue of your paramour," apologized Abraham in his haughtiest voice.

"That's more like it! Anyway, tell me more about the luscious Lincoln."

"He just so…perfect," gushed Abraham.

He had been rehashing every last second of his encounter with Lincoln ever since the previous Friday. Unfortunately, Topher had been away with his family over the weekend, so Abraham had been forced to obsess all alone.

"His smile…his voice…and the way he called me 'Beau'."

"Sounds like he *likes* you."

"Maybe he just calls everyone 'Beau'?"

"Possible, but unlikely. Besides, why wouldn't he mean it? You are pretty smoking hot, you know."

"Stop it."

Abraham felt a telltale tide of warmth sweep across his face. He'd never been comfortable taking compliments about his appearance.

"It's true…if only you weren't so damn *self-conscious*."

"I'm working on it," said Abraham, a tad defensively.

"I know, I know." He gave Abraham a friendly pat on the shoulder. "You deserve to have a boyfriend too."

"Thanks…I just wish I was outgoing as you," sighed Abraham.

"Well we can't all be perfect, mi amigo."

"Funny."

"So, why don't you ask him out?"

The suggestion set off a mini-whirlwind of worry in Abraham's brain.

"No, I couldn't…I mean what would I…No, I'd just be…"

"Incapable of finishing a sentence?"

Abraham lunged at Topher to give him a playful smack but his friend was far too quick and easily scooted out of the way – wrestling had given him a handy nimbleness. Admitting defeat, Abraham sat back and picked up the rest of his chicken salad.

"I could ask him for you?" offered Topher, before taking a large bite out his meatball sub.

"What are we in the fifth grade?"

"Just trying to help. We need to get that cherry of yours popped soon. Can't have you going off to college as a chaste, little virgin," teased Topher, light-heartedly.

"Ha! I appreciate your concern, but I need to grow some balls and do it myself."

"Don't let them get too big. I saw them in the showers last week and they're already huge!"

"Perve!"

"It's not my fault. You couldn't miss them, they were pendulous!"

This time Topher wasn't quick enough and Abraham managed to jab him sportingly in the chest. The bell rang and they hurriedly finished the remains of their lunches before heading back towards the classrooms, all the while continuing their friendly banter.

* * *

That Saturday afternoon found Abraham sitting diligently at his large mahogany desk, surrounded by books and attempting to be studious. It was only a few weeks into the term and he was already loaded down with an annoying amount of essays and readings. Staying focused on his homework, however, wasn't an easy feat, as the day was full of distractions. Through his bedroom window Abraham could hear all manner of neighborhood sounds – barking dogs, shrieking children and the rumble of a distant lawnmower or two. Momentarily giving up, Abraham crossed to the open window and took in the splendor of the bright, clear-skied, late summer's day. Down in his backyard, Abraham could see his Cocker Spaniel, Captain Reynolds – Cap for short – enthusiastically running around the swimming pool chasing invisible foes. He'd been named after Abraham's favorite character from Firefly, a popular sci-fi series, because of their similarly fearless attitudes and matching brown coats. They had gotten the energetic pup from Topher's mom – she owned the local veterinarian practice – three years ago and he was very much a cherished part of the family.

His attention was caught by the sounds of laughter and music wafting from next door. Abraham looked up over the back hedge and into the Deacons' backyard, where a bevy of beautiful men, around fifteen in total, were prancing about in revealing swimwear. There were a few other people wandering about, fiddling with pieces of lighting equipment, applying makeup and adjusting the swimwear. It was a sight Abraham had become well familiar with over the past few years, as his neighbors' backyard had often been the setting for photo shoots and promotional videos for CocKed underwear, the pool and garden providing a wonderful setting to show off their wares. Thad Deacon, one half of the married coupled who lived there, was a part-time underwear model for the brand – his long blonde surfer hair, hazel eyes and all over tan making him one of the more popular models. Shrewdly, the company also employed a variety of men, from twinks to muscle bears and every strapping variation in between – guaranteed to have something for everyone

It was without a doubt Abraham's preferred brand of undergarment, in fact, he had almost a hundred pairs. Not that he had an addiction exactly; rather, the signature, silk-lined crotch allowed him to feel a touch sexier than he gave himself credit for in real life. Abraham religiously watched their videos as soon as they were released on CocKed.com, with his music turned up loud and the bedroom door locked tight – his mother had nearly caught him in an indelicate situation once and it wasn't an experience that he longed to repeat. The videos weren't porn per se but with all the playful, manly grinding onto one another it wasn't a far way off of it.

Abraham recognized his all-time favorite models – Ali and Seb – sitting in the hot tub at the far side of the pool, looking rather cozy. Seb was the very picture of a Californian Beach Boy with bronzed skin, sun-bleached hair and striking blue eyes, while Ali had a swarthier complexion with a mop of curly dark hair and a muscular, hairy chest. Abraham loved when they were in shots together and he'd oft imagined himself between them, the very willing object of their affections.

Without realizing it, Abraham had begun to massage his growing erection through his denim shorts. He moved to the side of his window, as he didn't want to get caught touching himself while openly ogling the guys.

I don't want them to think I'm some sort of creepy stalker.

Opportunely, he was home alone so Abraham had no fear of being interrupted by his family. He slipped his hand inside the waistband of his shorts and then into his underwear, grabbing a firm hold of himself. His index finger slid over the top of his manhood, feeling the sticky wetness of his precum, as it leaked from his engorged cockhead.

Abraham gently bit his lower lip as he started to slowly jack his member to the sight of the tantalizingly close, glistening, male flesh. He pulled his hand out and undid his shorts, pushing them and his underwear down around his ankles. Taking himself in hand again, Abraham used his other hand to fondle his sensitive, and extremely full, balls. A light breeze came through the window and caressed his skin, as his hand began to pump faster and faster, until it became a blur of erotic movement.

He was so worked up that within a minute, his body tensed in anticipation and his breath began to come in short, sharp bursts. The thick, cloudy seed exploded from his throbbing manhood and onto the polished floorboards of Abraham's bedroom floor. Abraham grabbed a t-shirt from the nearby clothes hamper and cleaned first himself, and then the floor. Instead of pulling up his pants right away, Abraham continued watching the homoerotic display in the garden below. After only a few minutes Abraham's manhood began to re-inflate without his even touching it – not a surprising occurrence given his age and surging hormones.

Absentmindedly, Abraham reached down and once more gripped his increasingly hard member. This time, he used slow, firm, measured strokes. The urgency of the first release over, Abraham was in no hurry to shoot a second time. He stared intently at the oiled bodies as they frolicked by the pool, watching as their muscles contracted and released with each movement. Over the course of the next hour, a thoroughly mesmerized Abraham emptied his balls four more times, only stopping as his hand was starting to cramp and his manhood began to feel somewhat tender.

As much as Abraham had enjoyed the show he would have much preferred to have someone else helping to lighten his load and knew just whom he'd like to fill the position.

Lincoln.

Reluctantly, Abraham tossed the thoroughly soiled t-shirt into his laundry hamper and returned to his studies, although he would have much rather been in the pool with all the guys…even if he knew damn well that he'd be too shy and embarrassed to look them in the eye, let alone say anything to them. That aside, it was unlikely that Abraham would ever come face-to-face with one of the objects of his lust.

Only in my dreams.

* * *

A few days later, Abraham was running late to his biology class. Gingerly opening the door, Abraham saw his teacher, Mrs. Mears, standing in front of the blackboard, her piercing blue-gray eyes focused on the doorway through her horn-rimmed glasses. She had previously been Abraham's teacher for other science classes and he quite liked her, as she was far less stuffy and more relatable than the other teachers. Interestingly, there was quite a bit of debate amongst the senior class as to her actual age. Her relatively unlined, fine-featured face, cascading raven hair, and firm youthful-looking body – high school rumor had it that she was an extreme sports fan – was often the focus of interest, from both students and faculty alike.

Upon entering the room, Abraham noticed that everyone seemed to have moved from their usual benches and someone else was sitting in his regular spot. A look of confusion crossed his face and he turned back to Mrs. Mears for guidance.

"Ah, Mr. Chadwick, so good of you to join us," remarked Mrs. Mears, a faint German accent still present in her voice, despite having been in the States for well over two decades.

"Sorry," murmured Abraham, sheepishly.

"I've just assigned lab partners for the rest of term. Go take the place up the back by Mr. Shaw."

Mr. Shaw? No, it couldn't be…Lincoln?

Abraham looked towards the back of the classroom where he saw Lincoln, who had raised his hand and was beckoning him over. He couldn't believe his luck but then Abraham was hit with the entirely unnerving realization that he'd probably have to talk to his crush in a coherent manner. His heart sped up, so much so that Abraham was sure that the whole class must be able to hear it beating frantically inside his chest. He imagined their eyes boring into him, sensing his discomfort as he walked to the back of the classroom. Abraham took his place and as he sat down gave Lincoln the smallest of smiles, which was returned with interest.

"There will be five practical exams this semester…" began Mrs. Mears.

"Double Bee?" whispered Lincoln, offering up a bag of small, golden hard candy.

Abraham shook his head slightly and focused his attention to the front of the room. The rest of the class was trying for Abraham, struggling to listen to Mrs. Mears' instructions and doing his very best not to outright stare at his new lab partner, but he couldn't help stealing several furtive glances. Sitting so close to Lincoln, Abraham detected a faint hint of a pleasant, honey scent.

It must be all those candies he eats. He smells so good…I'll never be able to concentrate.

Eventually, the bell rang and released Abraham from his torture. As they stood up to go, Lincoln leaned in towards Abraham.

"So glad I got paired with ya, Beau," said Lincoln quietly. "I'm sure we'll have a whole lotta fun."

"Umm…yeah," mumbled Abraham, unsure of what his lab partner had meant.

And with that Lincoln headed off to his next class, leaving Abraham standing there like a bewildered deer. His mind spun with a billion questions, none of which he had an answer for.

What does he mean by that? Is he teasing me? Does he know that I like him?

* * *

Later that week, Abraham was skimming through the chlorinated water of the Olympic-sized, indoor swimming pool, located to the side of the gym at St. Francis Xavier. He'd been there for nearly an hour, as had the rest of the swimming squad, due to their upcoming swim meet. Thanks to his dedication and performance times, this year Abraham had been chosen to be co-captain of the St. Francis Xavier team, along with Tobias. The relationship between the lads was friendly enough but Tobias was the more outgoing and popular of the two by far. Not that Abraham was unpopular as such. Indeed, he was generally well liked but it was more that he was so quiet and shy that he just wasn't noticed in the same way. Tobias, on the other hand, was hard to miss. Apart from being quite attractive with sandy-blond hair, gentle brown eyes and a smooth tanned body, Tobias was also one of the tallest boys in the school, standing at six-foot-three. The other remarkable thing about him was the size of his appendage, which appeared to perfectly in proportion to his height; given the way it constantly appeared to strain the fabric of his swimwear to its very limit. Abraham had seen the manhood free-range in the showers and even in a non-aroused state it was quite something to behold. Naturally, it had made its way into Abraham's fantasies on occasion, even if the sheer size of it both enticed and scared him in equal measure.

As Abraham turned to do his final lap, with a great deal less energy than when he'd started, he could hear Coach Noah

Whiting's voice shouting out various instructions to his squad. The booming baritone was easily heard over the splashing and general noise around the pool. Abraham was terribly fond of his coach. He'd nurtured Abraham's talent and encouraged him, not taking any notice of his shyness and forcing Abraham to train harder and perform even better than the young swimmer thought he could. The coach was a ruggedly handsome man in his early thirties and had been the subject of one of Abraham's earliest crushes – and rather a few wet dreams. Easily understandable after the attention he'd shown Abraham, although his jet-black hair, ever-present five-o'clock shadow, sharp gray-green eyes, hairy chest and well-developed build certainly contributed to the attraction. Not that the coach had been anything other than professional during their time together – much to Abraham's disappointment.

Abraham finished his lap and wearily climbed out of the pool. He retrieved his large yellow towel from the hooks by the door and began to dry himself off, as Coach Whiting came over to talk to him.

"Good job, Chadwick. You and Tobias keep those times up and we'll smash them at Regionals!"

"Thanks, Coach."

"OK, you're done for the day. Rest up and I'll see you tomorrow afternoon."

Wrapping his towel around his shoulders, Abraham began to walk along the length of the pool towards the change rooms. As usual, the stands by the pool were half-full of students laughing and generally hanging about. Some were friends with the swimmers and some came purely for the eye-candy factor, as all members of the squad, both male and female, were in fantastic shape. A fact unquestionably accentuated by their ever-so-snug red and blue swimwear.

Abraham was halfway along the pool when a flash of red caught his attention and he saw that Lincoln was in attendance – wearing his vibrantly colored sneakers. He was sitting in amongst a raucous group of seniors, made up primarily of cheerleading crew members, including Tobias' girlfriend Lydia, a petite lass with pretty, hazel eyes and curly brunette shoulder-length hair. Lincoln himself was dressed in the St. Francis Xavier cheerleader outfit of a fitted blue t-shirt and white track pants with red piping.

He must have made the squad at tryouts yesterday.

It hadn't escaped Abraham's attention that Lincoln had become rather popular in his short time at the school. Abraham wasn't all that surprised, considering Lincoln's good looks and friendly demeanor. Lincoln was chatting enthusiastically with Austin, one of the few other boys on the cheerleading squad. Abraham didn't know Austin well but had long admired his athletic frame and strong, pleasing features.

Lincoln stood up suddenly, apparently in the midst of telling a hilarious story, judging by the laughter and animated faces of the group. Abraham appreciated the way Lincoln's track pants clung to his lower half as he moved, pulling taut up against the solid, muscular legs contained within. He also couldn't help but notice the way they sat around Lincoln's crotch, highlighting the uninhibited movement of an apparently considerable member beneath the material. The very thought of it caused Abraham to trip over his own feet but he quickly regained his balance and avoided embarrassing himself entirely.

I'm such an idiot!

He quickly made his way towards the change room door but as he was about to enter, Abraham looked over his shoulder for one last glimpse of Lincoln. Just as Abraham turned in his direction, Lincoln looked up and their eyes connected.

Damn it! Now he probably thinks I'm a stalker.

It came as a complete surprise to Abraham that instead of showing disdain at Abraham's gaze, Lincoln smiled and waved at him. At first, Abraham thought he must have been gesturing to someone else and quickly looked around but found that he was the only one there. Abraham shyly waved back and disappeared into the change rooms, where he was immediately engulfed by a wave of happiness. When Abraham caught sight of himself in the mirrors over the sinks, he wasn't particularly shocked to see that he was blushing with a contented smile playing upon his lips.

Could he really like me? Am I deluding myself? Damn he looked good in those track pants!

* * *

Midway through the following week, Abraham found himself in front of the blackboard in the biology lab, giving a brief report on the circulatory system of dolphins to his extremely bored-looking classmates. Abraham was nearing the end of his short, yet informative, speech when he started to feel strangely cold. He looked down and saw, to his growing horror, that he was without a stitch of clothing to protect his modesty. The sniggers of his classmates filled his ears and Abraham felt his face burn with shame and he was afraid to raise his head.

Not this dream again!

It was a nightmare he'd had on and off for years, although he knew it was a fairly common anxiety dream amongst teenagers. All of a sudden the laughing ceased and Abraham's head snapped back up, only to see that the classroom was empty; except for one solitary figure sitting up the back, Lincoln.

Lincoln stood up and came out from behind the bench and Abraham could see that he was completely naked as well. He walked slowly towards Abraham, his impressive manhood swinging side to side in a mesmerizing fashion with every step. In the blink of an eye, Lincoln was standing directly in front of Abraham, their faces barely an inch apart.

Well, this is new...I might as well take advantage of it.

Showing courage, he wouldn't have in real life, Abraham closed the gap between them and kissed Lincoln with a sense of urgent longing. Lincoln kissed him back, his hands gripping tightly onto Abraham's back pulling him in even closer. Abraham enjoyed the slight, sugary taste of honey in the kiss, while he ran his hands down to Lincoln's enticingly round buttocks.

They broke apart and Abraham was unsure what to do next. Lincoln promptly solved the problem by kissing his way down Abraham's body. The dream was so vivid that Abraham could actually feel the heat of Lincoln's breath on his naked torso, as he moved downwards.

Moments later, Lincoln's face was level with Abraham's rock-hard erection, which was gushing a veritable fountain of precum and forming a small puddle on the floor. Lincoln took a firm hold of Abraham's manhood in his right hand and moved his head forward. Abraham held his breath in anticipation, desperately wanting to feel the sensation of Lincoln swallowing him whole. Just as Lincoln's inviting mouth was about to make contact with the sticky cockhead, Abraham abruptly ejaculated, sending thick white cream splattering all over Lincoln's face and into his open mouth.

Abraham woke up in his bed with a start, his heart beating wildly and a little breathless. He was a little disorientated at first but soon realized what had happened. He reached down with his right hand and touched the very sticky crotch of his pajamas.

Why couldn't I have held off a bit longer? Dammit!

He wriggled out of his damp pajama bottoms and threw them to the floor, but couldn't be bothered getting out of the warm embrace of his bed to put fresh ones on. Besides, he rather liked the feeling of the cotton sheets against his bare flesh. Abraham knew he'd have to drop his stained sheets and pajamas into the washing machine in the morning to clean away the evidence of his nocturnal emissions. Knowingly, his parents hadn't asked why when Abraham had started doing his own laundry a few years back and the three of them had been saved from having a very awkward conversation.

Abraham lay back down and attempted to drift off to sleep again – hoping to continue where he left off. Unfortunately, he was still too worked up by his dream and became lost in his turbulent thoughts about Lincoln instead. Abraham would have loved to be as confident as he was in the dream; taking control and seducing Lincoln, but he knew that is was purely the stuff of fantasy and unlikely to become reality at any point in the near future.

If only.

* * *

That weekend, Abraham received a completely unexpected, yet not unwelcome, surprise. Lazing on one of the sun lounges by the pool, Abraham reveled in the glorious sunshine of the day, after having finished his tiring morning routine of fifty laps. The heady scent of gardenias wafted from the Walker's garden next door, carried by a gentle breeze that ruffled the water and ran across Abraham's drying body. His skin was lightly bronzed; a color he'd had to work for most of the summer to achieve… thanks to his mother's Irish heritage getting any sort of tan had always been a challenge.

His faithful companion, Captain Reynolds, was curled up on the grassy area by the patio and lightly snoring, evidently enjoying his time in the sun as well. Laying face down on the small table by his side was a battered-looking copy of Abraham's all-time favorite Stephen King novel – Carrie – not that he harbored desires to set fire to his fellow classmates at the Prom…well not most days. Abraham was about halfway through it, for the tenth time, but the warmth of the day had caused his eyes to become gradually heavier, so he'd put the book down.

Just for a minute.

Abraham was in a state of pleasant half-dozing when he heard the familiar sounds of clicking metal as the side gate opened and closed. Given the day and the time, he figured it was Andre, the pool cleaner, who worked for Poolside Pride. It was a small company owned by his neighbor, Thad Deacon, who took care of pretty much all the pools in the local area – it turned out the underwear model was also quite an astute businessman. Abraham lazily opened his eyes and began to sit up.

"Hi, An…" He stopped mid sentence, shocked by the appearance of the least likely person in his backyard. "Lincoln?"

"Heya, Abe!" greeted Lincoln in his syrupy Southern drawl. "I didn't know this was your place."

Abraham couldn't have been more surprised if Captain Reynolds had sat up and started to recite Shakespeare.

"Umm…yeah…what happened to Andre?"

"He's off on vacation…to Canada, I think. I only just started with the company, so not too sure. 'Fraid you're stuck with little ol' me. Hope ya aren't too disappointed, Beau."

There's nothing little about him!

"Yes…no…I mean…OK. I'll be back."

Flustered in the extreme, Abraham scurried back inside the house with an almost superhuman speed. His dreams about Lincoln had continued to become more explicit over the past week and to see the object of his lust standing right there in his own backyard had flooded Abraham's system with an unsettling mixture of excitement and terror. Through the glass door that led out to the patio, Abraham could see Lincoln disappear into the small shed that contained all the pool cleaning supplies.

What am I doing? I'm hiding from him? What the fuck is wrong with me? Why does his accent have to be so sexy?

Lincoln soon emerged with the pool scoop in hand and moved towards the sun lounge where Abraham had been lying. He stripped off his t-shirt, leaving him only wearing a pair of temptingly small, faded denim shorts, and then began his toil. Abraham was transfixed, as Lincoln's muscles gently strained as he went about his work, scooping the leaves from the pool. In particular, Abraham's eyes were drawn to a crescent shaped scar on Lincoln's

24

upper arm that undulated as the triceps muscles contracted beneath it. The small mark only served to add to Lincoln's appeal.

Even his imperfections are perfect! Erghh I'm so sappy! Go talk to him!

Eventually, after a great deal of internal debate, Abraham forced himself to go back outside and talk to the object of his affection.

"I thought ya abandoned me!" Lincoln exclaimed a tad melodramatically.

"Nah, I just needed to do something inside."

"My apologies then, kind sir. I shoulda known you'd never leave me."

Lincoln then gave him a wide smile and playful wink, which only served to perturb Abraham further. As Abraham sat back down on the sun lounge he tried to relax and read his book but he kept finding his gaze drift back in the direction of the handsome new pool boy. After a few minutes, Abraham came to the unpleasant realization that he was becoming very prominently aroused – his sea-green Speedos didn't leave a lot the imagination at the best of times – so he quickly turned around to sit on the side of the lounge, putting the book down to cover his crotch. He started to reapply the sunscreen to his shoulders and neck but was having trouble covering his back.

"Do ya need some help with the cream?" offered Lincoln.

Yes, I'd love you to cream me!

"Umm…sure…thanks."

"Can't have that fine skin of yours getting burnt, now."

Abraham handed him the bottle and put his hands down in front of him, keeping the book in place to conceal his ever-growing erection. Lincoln sat down behind Abraham almost touching but not quite. Abraham shivered as Lincoln squeezed a big dollop of the sun cream onto his back.

"Too cold?"

"Nah, it's OK."

Abraham stifled a moan as Lincoln placed his strong hands onto the middle of Abraham's back and began to rub in the cream using deliberate strokes. It was closest they'd ever been and Abraham was doing his very best not to hyperventilate. His nipples began to harden and several beads of sweat appeared on his forehead.

"Ya doing, OK?" asked Lincoln, with a note of concern in his voice.

"Yea...yes. Why?"

"Ya just seem kinda tense, is all."

He can tell! Oh God!

"It's a...it's probably just from training. I didn't really stretch today after my laps."

"Ya really looked great in the pool."

"What?"

He's been watching me?

"The other day at training. It was almost like ya were flying through the water. I'm more like a floundering whale when I try."

The self-depreciating tone endeared Lincoln to Abraham even more and he felt himself relax ever-so-slightly in his crush's company.

"I doubt that."

"It's true! I sure wish I could move like ya do."

Lincoln appeared to be brazenly flirting but Abraham's lack of confidence made him question the pool boy's motives.

Maybe he just wants a bigger tip. He couldn't be interested in me. Why would he be when he could have his pick of the guys...or girls.

Lincoln was sitting so close that Abraham could feel the edges of his hot breath against his back, as he continued to rub in the cream. It seemed to Abraham that Lincoln was taking his time with the task at hand. The large, strong hands moved lower and lower down Abraham's back, firmly massaging as they went.

"It's just a matter of...you just need to..."

Abraham's senses were in overdrive, making it ridiculously hard to concentrate, as Lincoln's natural musky scent – enhanced by his perspiration – wafted around them. Every fiber of Abraham's body yearned to turn around fall into a passionate embrace with Lincoln.

Wanting to do the pool boy? Am I in a seventies porno? Get a grip!

"...you just have to practice is all," said Abraham, finally getting his sentence out.

"I guess, but I find it much easier to move on land. Pikes, tumbles and somersaults sure, but butterfly and breaststroke not so much."

"Everyone has their own talents."

"I bet ya got lots of talents, Beau."

The compliment went straight to Abraham's head and it was all he could do to refrain from jumping up and down in joyful exhilaration. Lincoln had finished rubbing in the cream but his hands still hadn't left Abraham's back. They were resting on the bare skin just above the line of his swimwear and the pleasing warmth of them all but drove Abraham to distraction. Abraham felt separated from the rest of the world, all the neighborhood sounds had faded away and all he could hear was his own breathing. His manhood threatened to burst out of his swimwear completely. Thankfully, Abraham was soon released from his exquisite torture.

"Well, it's been mighty nice chatting but I should get back to it. Let me know if I can do anything else for ya," said Lincoln suggestively, as he got up from the sun lounge.

"Yeah...I will, thanks. What would I have done without you?"

What did I just say? Am I insane? Stop being such an idiot!

Lincoln simply smiled and went back to fetch the pool scoop. Abraham felt like his face must be crimson with humiliation. He stayed facing away until he heard Lincoln resume his work and then quickly laid face down on the lounge to hide his unruly appendage. Abraham would have absolutely died if Lincoln had seen how turned on he was, although at his age even a stiff breeze could trigger a raging erection.

A short while later, Lincoln finished up and packed away the equipment back into the shed. Abraham was torn in his desires. On one hand he wanted Lincoln to stay close but he was also in desperate need of relief.

"See ya Monday, Beau."

"Yeah, see you then."

As soon as he heard the gate lock again, Abraham raced upstairs, ripped off his swimwear and jumped into the shower. The hot water beat down on his tensed body, as he capably took himself in hand – Lincoln at very forefront of his imagining. It took all of thirty frantic seconds of jacking before Abraham's seed spurted upwards and onto the white tiled wall. He gasped with the intensity of the orgasm, as waves of pleasure wracked his body. When he'd recovered, Abraham made sure to carefully wash away the remnants of his ejaculation; he didn't want to leave any unpleasant surprises for his family, after all. As Abraham padded down the hallway to his bedroom, with a fluffy towel wrapped around his waist, his thoughts were still fully dominated by Lincoln.

If only I had the courage. What, I'm the cowardly lion, now? Why can't I just tell him how I feel?

* * *

The bleachers were packed to overflowing with keen spectators – a rowdy mix of students, parents and teachers – waving banners, cheering and having a gay old time of it. It was hard not to become wrapped up in the cult-like chants and bubbling enthusiasm of the crowd. Seated smack bang in the middle of the stands, Abraham took in the proceedings with Topher faithfully by his side. Below them the field was full of tired and sweaty football players meandering about congratulating one another. The Homecoming Game had finished only moments beforehand and St. Francis Xavier was celebrating their triumphant win over their most hated rivals – All Saints. Abraham wasn't a huge fan of football and while ostensibly he'd gone along to show school spirit, the main reason he'd braved the hordes was the prospect of seeing Lincoln performing with the cheerleading squad – something he'd been looking forward to all week.

The cheerleaders had put on quite the show at halftime with many feats of acrobatic strength and skill, although Abraham's focus had been somewhat contained to a specific individual. Every time Abraham saw Lincoln showing off his physical prowess, like tossing a fellow cheerleader up into the air or doing the splits, his jeans got that extra bit tighter. Fortunately, he had his jacket across his lap, covering his growing bulge. The squad was now in the process of doing an impromptu victory routine, in order to rev up the crowd even further.

"Fuck, your boy can move," remarked Topher.

"He's not my boy," replied Abraham, more defensive than he'd meant to.

"Oooh, touchy," taunted Topher. "Goddamn, I bet he'd be awesome to fuck."

"Topher! You've got Eli."

"So. Doesn't mean I can't imagine what Lincoln would look like bouncing up and down on my…"

"Shut up! I don't want to hear it," snapped Abraham.

"Sorry. I was just having fun."

Seeing the look of hurt on Topher's face, Abraham felt mean-spirited. He knew full well that Topher was only messing around but Abraham's longing for Lincoln was playing with his mind. Abraham adopted an apologetic tone and smiled.

"No, I'm sorry. I'm getting stupid over nothing. Ogle away."

"Nah, it's all good. I've got Austin in my sights now!" Topher joked with an impish grin.

"I don't know how Eli puts up with you."

"He loves me! Besides he's just as bad. You should hear some of the things he says about the guys on the football team."

"Then you're both debauched."

"Don't be such a prude," teased Topher, lightheartedly.

"I'm trying."

"Don't worry, with my careful instruction, we'll have you hosting orgies in no time at all."

"Gee, thanks. I can hardly wait."

Even though sarcasm dripped from his every word, Abraham's manhood involuntarily hardened at the thought of being at the center of a pile of writhing male bodies.

All those mouths and…

He shook himself out of his daydream, readjusted his jacket and tried to focus on the festivities.

Once the cheerleaders had finished with their latest burst of peppiness, attention turned to the small stage, which had been erected on the opposite side of the football field, facing the bleachers. All the Head Teachers were seated upon it, along with the Homecoming King and Queen dressed in their ceremonial capes and crowns. Unsurprisingly, an overwhelming majority had elected Jonas and Penny, the star quarterback and the captain of the cheerleading squad respectively, to their regal roles. They were one of the school's most popular – not to mention overly dramatic – couples. The status of their on-again-off-again relationship was always a hot subject for gossip. They were unquestionably the reigning monarchs of the school, with their cookie-cutter, model-perfect looks and forceful personalities. It was generally accepted that they'd win the titles of Prom King and Queen without any competition in May.

The King and Queen stood before the microphone and were taking turns delivering a somewhat formulaic speech to end the proceedings.

"Thanks for coming out and supporting the team and we wish everyone a Happy Homecoming!" squealed Penny.

"Go, Bears!" Jonas added complete with an obligatory fist pump.

Abraham and Topher dutifully applauded with the overly enthusiastic crowd – one could practically feel the infectious presence of school pride in the air. The bleachers began to steadily empty out as the spectators headed off to the parking lot. As they passed the end of the field, Abraham saw Lincoln chatting with some of the other cheerleaders.

Over the past few weeks, Abraham had discovered that the object of his desire was a man of many talents and something of an overachiever. Not that Abraham was stalking him exactly, but the school grapevine could be awfully handy at times. In addition to being a very capable member of the cheerleading squad, Lincoln was also on the debate team and a welcome new addition to the Glee club – his deeper timbre had been desperately missing from the female-heavy group.

Apparently sensing Abraham's gaze, Lincoln looked up and gave a friendly wave, which Abraham timidly returned.

"Go on over and talk to him," urged Topher.

"Nah, I don't want to intrude."

"Fine…Chicken."

"I just can't."

"OK…well don't blame me when you die a virgin with only Captain Reynolds by your side."

"Thanks," grumbled Abraham, only half-offended.

"My pleasure. Alright, let's go find my beary boyfriend."

The pair soon located Eli coming out of the change rooms and the three headed off to Topher's compact, yellow hatchback.

When they arrived at the car they saw Tobias and Lydia climbing into a black 4WD parked next to them.

"Hey, you guys going to Austin's party tonight?" called Tobias through the open driver's side window.

"Sure are! We've just gotta swing by home and grab some supplies from my brother," answered Eli, a cheeky grin lighting his face.

The supplies in question were several six-packs and a bottle of vodka. Eli's older brother, Joshua, was always a willing accomplice when it came to party time shenanigans.

"Great, see you there!"

"Bye, boys," giggled Lydia, who sounded like she may have already started partaking of the festive cheer.

Even though Abraham was often invited to the popular parties, they weren't the most comfortable of social situations for him. With a good helping of liquid courage, however, Abraham was usually able to overcome his wallflower tendencies and make the effort to be social. They quickly clambered into the hatchback and the trio was soon off on their merry way, once they'd managed to escape the gridlock of cars all trying to leave the lot at the same time, of course.

* * *

A few weeks later, Abraham was seated at his bench in biology class patiently awaiting the results of the previous day's pop quiz that Mrs. Mears was in the process of handing back. A vaguely acrid chemical smell seemed to be seeping in from the physics lab next door.

Abraham wasn't too worried as he fairly sure that he did well in the test, a suspicion that was soon confirmed when Mrs.

Mears handed back his paper with a large A+ written on the top right-hand corner.

"Well done, Abraham." Then she moved towards Lincoln. "Unfortunately, the same can't be said for you Mr. Shaw. Perhaps some extra effort would be helpful." Her voice wasn't unkind but there was a tinge of disappointment to it.

Seeing Lincoln's face fall in despair as he looked at his test, Abraham felt an immediate wave of sympathy for his lab partner. The past weeks of working together in class and seeing Lincoln on the weekends, when he came to clean the pool, had helped Abraham to become slightly more at ease in his company. He could even manage coherent sentences around Lincoln without an instant erection…most of the time.

The bell rang, signaling the end of the period, and the students began to leave the room in a noisy rumble. Abraham quickly packed up his belongings and was getting up to go when he noticed that Lincoln was still sitting there, staring morosely at his returned test.

"Are you OK?" asked Abraham, his voice full of genuine concern.

"Nope. I got a D!" Lincoln looked completely miserable. "My momma is gonna to kill me! She said if I don't get at least a B average she's gonna to take away my Jeep until graduation!"

"That's rough."

"I don't get this stuff. I've really tried to understand it but it just won't stick in my head."

He sounded utterly defeated and Abraham's heart went out to him. Fighting an urge to console Lincoln with a hug, Abraham did his best to comfort his forlorn lab partner.

"I'm sure if you just study a bit harder you'll get it," encouraged Abraham.

Lincoln turned to face Abraham properly, his eyes full of hope.

"Would ya be keen to blow me?"

Abraham nearly fell over in shock.

"I'm sorry, *what*?"

"Would ya be keen to tutor me?" repeated Lincoln.

Did I really think he'd ask that? I really need a boyfriend...or some therapy.

"I don't know. I've never done that before."

While the idea of being all alone in a room with Lincoln certainly had appeal, Abraham was worried that it may make his infatuation worse and cause him to do something completely insane...like declaring his ever-lasting love.

"Please, Abe. Ya obviously know the stuff. I can't pay much but I'd be ever so grateful."

Abraham looked into Lincoln's pleading, hazelnut-brown eyes and felt all resistance dissolve away into the ether.

I'd do anything he wanted.

"OK, I'll do it," agreed Abraham, only a tiny bit of misgiving in his thoughts

"Thanks, man! You're really saving my ass."

That's not all I want to do to it.

Keeping his inner desires firmly to himself, Abraham replied. "No problem."

Lincoln clapped Abraham firmly on the shoulder and gave him a stunning white smile. Abraham loved the feel of Lincoln's strong hand squeezing his shoulder and foolishly wished he'd never let go.

It was then that Lincoln apparently noticed that they were all alone.

"Oops, I really gotta get to practice. How's tomorrow night?"

"For what?" asked Abraham, a quizzical expression clouding his face.

"Tutoring? Ya just said…"

I am SO stupid!

Abraham desperately wished that a highly localized earthquake would split the floor and let him disappear. Putting aside his mortification, he pulled himself together enough to finish the conversation.

"Oh, yeah, yeah…sure. Tomorrow's good for me. 'Round seven?"

"Perfect. See ya then, Beau."

What am I getting myself into? Does he want to spend more time with me or is it just for study? Of course, it's for study! Why would he want me? But he calls me Beau. I've got to stop deluding myself.

Abraham's thoughts zipped around his head for the rest of the afternoon but brought him no closer to any conclusions. Fortunately, he was saved from doing any further heavy thinking on the subject after school, by a grueling swim session followed by having to draft an essay on the Doomsday Clock for his Modern History class.

* * *

Despite Abraham's misgivings and growing inner turmoil, his first tutoring session with Lincoln had come and gone without incident. Lincoln had been a most attentive student with an obvious desire to learn the material, which had allowed

Abraham to temporarily put aside his feelings of lust and longing – for the most part – and focus instead on helping his lab partner. Not to say, that there hadn't been a fervent bout of self-pleasuring after the lesson, on Abraham's behalf, as soon as Lincoln had departed.

The weather became exceedingly gray and stormy for the rest of the week, which had in turn provided the perfect ambiance for that Friday night – Halloween. This year's must-attend party was being held at Tobias' house, as, his wonderfully easy-going parents had headed away for the weekend to let the kids have their fun – not a fact that Abraham had shared with his own parents.

What they don't know won't hurt me.

As usual, Topher and Eli were accompanying Abraham there. Abraham was always grateful for the escort, but he tended to wander off on his own after an hour or so, as he didn't want to become a third wheel. All three had put a great deal of effort into their outfits for the evening. Abraham had disguised himself as Captain Reynolds – the character rather than his dog – although he fully anticipated more than a few puzzled looks towards his meticulously put-together costume of a long brown jacket, red shirt and suspendered pants. Sadly, not everyone was a fan of sci-fi, after all. Topher was dressed as Han Solo – their shared geekiness was one of the rocks of their friendship. Unsurprisingly, Eli had gone as Han's perfect companion – Chewbacca…Eli did so love his furry costumes.

The trio arrived to a house ablaze with lights and the soft thump of muffled music coming through the walls. Abraham pressed firmly on the buzzer, unsure if it would be heard over the music blaring inside. His concern was proved unwarranted as the cobweb-covered front door soon swung open to reveal a bare-chested Tobias, dressed appropriately as Poseidon – given his dominance in the pool. He looked resplendent with his golden trident and matching crown, and a sheer aqua sarong that didn't do a great deal to hide the huge appendage swinging free beneath it. Abraham did his very best to keep his eyes upward.

"Greetings, fellow revelers! Come eat, drink and get wasted!" declared Tobias in a deep, roaring voice.

"Thanks, Tobi...I mean Lord Poseidon," responded Abraham respectfully.

He then gave a small, good-humored bow, infused with a great deal of mock reverence, which was promptly copied by both Eli and Topher. They walked into hallway and were confronted with a heaving sea of teenagers, in a myriad of colorful costumes and varying stages of inebriation, flowing throughout the house. As they dropped off the drinks and snacks they'd brought into the kitchen, Abraham caught a waft of smoke – tobacco mixed with something distinctly more herbal – coming through the open windows from the backyard. Taking a beer each, the lads then joined in the festivities, happily mingling with the crowd of creatures.

Around an hour later, Abraham was headed back to refill his drink when he unexpectedly bumped into Lincoln, who was on his way out of the kitchen and wearing a costume that Abraham knew well.

"Abe!" Lincoln shoved a glass full of bright blue liquid into Abraham's hand. "Have a Blue Zombie! I made 'em myself, we used to have it all the time back home."

"Thanks." He took a sip of the sugary blue concoction and coughed a little at the strength of the alcohol. "Delicious."

"There's a whole bowl of it in the kitchen, if ya want more."

They were standing terrifically close together in the doorway as people squeezed past them. Abraham enjoyed the nearness of Lincoln's body but was once again afraid his nerves may make him say something stupid. He also could have happily stared into Lincoln's soulful brown eyes all night without uttering a word, but didn't want to come across as some sort of freak.

"Captain Reynolds, right?" asked Lincoln.

"That's right." Abraham was surprised that Lincoln had guessed correctly and that he was wearing just as equally geeky an outfit. "And you're Captain Jack Harkness?"

"Damn, Beau. I'm glad ya got it. Everyone's been asking why I'm some random old-fashioned soldier? Don't y'all watch Doctor Who up here?"

We have more in common than I thought. Maybe I'm not deluding myself.

"Yeah, people haven't really had an idea who I'm supposed to be either."

"Geeks unite!" toasted Lincoln.

They clinked their plastic glasses together in solidarity. Abraham's face was lit up by a wide smile. Seizing the opportunity, Abraham decided to try and build on their unanticipated shared fondness for all things geeky.

"Have you been to Geek HQ in the city? It's got a huge range of comics and memorabilia, especially Doctor Who and…"

All of sudden, Abraham was interrupted by a squealing cheerleader in a cat costume, Annika, who seemed to be in exceptionally good spirits. When sober, she was a pretty, ice-cold blonde, who could've easily filled the role of a Hitchcockian heroine. Now, however, her natural grace was missing as she clumsily bumped into the pair and then practically jumped on Lincoln to demand his immediate attention.

"Lincoln! We're having a dance off out on the terrace. You've gotta come!" commanded Annika, her words more than a little slurred.

"How could I possibly refuse such a kind invitation, my dear?" Lincoln gave Abraham a shrug and an apologetic smile. "Catch ya later, Beau!"

Feeling disappointed, Abraham watched them go, all the while having some very uncharitable thoughts towards Annika. He downed his Blue Zombie and his body immediately flooded with comforting warmth. After a brief pit stop in the kitchen for another hit of the strong blue cocktail, Abraham wandered about the house feeling decidedly tipsy and watching his fellow students becoming progressively drunker. Not that he was standing apart from the action by any means. The alcohol coursing through his system had stripped away his inhibitions and had made Abraham very chatty indeed.

A few pleasantly social hours passed with his fellow revelers and Abraham was heading back to the kitchen for yet another top up when a familiar figure crashed into him.

"Sorry, Abe," mumbled a very inebriated Cassidy, captain of the wrestling team and Eli's best friend.

Abraham had known him since grade school and the pair had always gotten along reasonably well. But then again, Abraham wasn't the type who drew enemies. As well as being an all-round good guy, Cassidy was quite an appealing specimen, with messy blond-streaked brown hair, startling blue eyes, a short but solid muscular build and pale skin, which was highlighted by his adorably rosy-red cheeks. Tonight, he was dressed as Tarzan, in a tattered brown loincloth, which more than showed off his hard-won wrestling physique.

"Have you seen Cheetah?" asked Cassidy, a look of distress passing over his face.

"What?"

"Cheetah…my monkey! I had him wrapped around my neck but now I can't find him."

Abraham hazarded a guess that he was talking about a toy one rather than a live wild animal but you never knew.

The poor guy. I should try and be helpful.

"No, I don't think so. Where did you last see him?"

"I…umm…I don't…" Cassidy looked slightly lost for a second as his eyes glazed over but he soon snapped back to the conversation. "Having a good night?"

"Yeah, it's been OK."

"You're looking damn fine!"

Is he hitting on me now?

Ordinarily, Abraham would have been flattered but in his present state Cassidy wasn't at his most attractive. Cassidy had come out as bisexual around a year ago and had dated his way through a fair number of their fellow classmates. Indeed, at times it'd seemed like he and Eli had been locked in a fierce competition to be named the school bike – a title Cassidy had won by default when Eli had given up his wanton ways for the love of Topher.

"Umm, thanks you too," replied Abraham awkwardly.

"You wanna go...you wanna...ah, I don't feel so good."

Cassidy had begun weaving noticeably from side to side and Abraham wasn't quite sure what to do.

"Do you want me to find Eli?" offered Abraham.

"Nah...umm...can you...I think I'm going to hurl."

"OK, come with me."

Taking Cassidy's hand, Abraham managed to maneuver the poor drunken wrestler to the downstairs bathroom, which was thankfully unoccupied. Cassidy rushed forward to the toilet and sunk to his knees. Abraham quickly stepped back outside to give Cassidy his privacy – and avoid seeing the messy result of his over consumption. He then swiftly headed to the nearby fridge to grab a bottle of water for his sickly friend.

A slightly less drunk-looking Cassidy sheepishly reemerged from the bathroom a few minutes afterwards.

"Doing, OK?" asked Abraham, as he handed Cassidy the water.

"Yeah...I'm feeling much better." He took the bottle and gratefully chugged it down. "Thanks, bro. You're the best!"

Cassidy gave Abraham a big, strong bear hug and then he half-stumbled off outside, presumably to continue his partying.

Better him than me.

Abraham surveyed the drunken crowd and began to contemplate heading homewards when someone unexpectedly grabbed him from behind.

"You're all mine now, brown coat!"

Abraham wriggled out of his assailant's grasp and turned to find a somewhat intoxicated Topher.

"Hey, drunky. I'm probably going to get going," explained Abraham.

"Like hell you are! I just came to find you to play Spin the Bottle."

"Ah, no. I don't think so."

"Come on, it'll be fun!" exclaimed Topher, in a distantly convincing manner.

"It's not really my thing. Anyway, I have training tomorrow and…"

Obviously realizing that he was losing, Topher cut Abraham off with his trump card.

"Lincoln's playing and he's dressed as Captain Jack!"

The pair had long ago confessed their mutual desire of bedding the fictional character. The possibly of getting to kiss his crush and indulge in one of his other fantasies was too good an opportunity for Abraham to ignore.

"Yeah, I saw him before…OK! Lead the way, Han."

"Knew that'd get you!"

Topher led Abraham upstairs to their host's bedroom, where Tobias' interests were clearly on display – posters of bikini-clad beauties adorned the walls and a large wooden bookshelf was lined with swimming trophies. A boisterous group of partygoers were sitting around the edges of the queen-sized bed. There was an atmosphere of high sexual tension and expectation, no doubt helped along by the fairly erotic display happening in the middle of the bed. The stars of the scintillating show were Annika and her best friend Kathryn, a robust girl with an athletic build and friendly brown eyes, who was also dressed as a similarly, skimpily-clad cat. Kathryn was keenly nibbling on Annika's neck while their friends cheered, although rumor had it that this wasn't exactly unusual behavior for the two cheerleaders.

The boys waited until the girls had finished before they squeezed in between Eli and Lydia, who made a very fetching Wonder Woman. Next to her was Jonas, in Roman gladiator garb, and Penny, with a black wig covering her habitual bleach-blond bob and looking vaguely Egyptian. It took Abraham a second to work out who the Homecoming King and Queen were supposed to be.

Antony and Cleopatra! Well they do suit the roles of ill-fated lovers. Stop being a bitch!

On the far side of the bed, beside Lincoln, was yet another member of the cheerleading crew, Austin, who was disguised as a surprisingly sexy zombie. To their right sat Tobias with a goofy grin upon his face and slightly glassy eyes.

Looks like the King of the Oceans has been drinking like a fish.

Abraham put his increased catty thoughts down to his alcohol consumption and decided to focus on the game instead. He saw that there was a cell phone in the center of the bed with the words 'BITE' and 'NECK' flashing on the screen. While Abraham knew of the app version of the game he'd never played it – or the traditional one for the matter.

"Your turn, Jonas!" exclaimed Penny in a shrill tone.

Obligingly, Jonas leaned forward and gave the phone a mighty twist. The image of a multicolored bottle flashed on the screen as it spun around and around. It slowly came to rest with a flashing arrow pointing directly at Lydia and the words 'KISS' and 'PUBLIC' illuminated. Lydia turned to Jonas and they indulged in a very passionate seeming kiss, as the group around them became even more animated and cheered them on. Abraham was a little puzzled as to why neither Tobias nor Penny seemed to be particularly disturbed by their respective partners kissing.

If it was my boyfriend I wouldn't be so calm. Maybe I am a prude?

After a minute or so the kiss ended and the phone was spun again. This time it was Eli and Penny who were paired together, with the instructions to spend two minutes alone in private – Tobias' walk-in closet had been chosen for the purpose. They obediently went to their fate as the all-powerful phone demanded.

"Doesn't it bother you?" whispered Abraham to Topher.

"Nah, it's all good fun. Loosen up!"

Before too long, the pair emerged from the closet, to the cheers and shouts of the group, their costumes slightly askew. They moved back to the bed and rejoined the others, and it was now Abraham's turn to spin the phone. He was filled with a confusing sensation of excitement and dread, as he reached over and sent the phone off on its twirling way.

Please let it be Lincoln.

Abraham's pulse raced as the cell phone spun and flashed, he honestly didn't know whether he wanted to run away or see what the fates had in store. For a moment it seemed as if his silent prayers had been answered as the phone slowed down in the vicinity of Lincoln. Abraham tried to keep himself from grinning like an idiot, as he didn't want to expose his hidden desires to the group. As it turned out, Abraham's worry was for nothing as the phone sailed past Lincoln and stopped dead in front of

Tobias, and indicated that they too were due for some time in the closet, but their assignation was to be much longer.

Ten minutes! What will we do in there? Tobias is straight!

Apparently sensing Abraham's worry, Topher quickly leaned in and whispered in his ear.

"It'll be fine. You can probably just chat about lap times or something."

Feeling less than reassured, Abraham dutifully got up and followed Tobias into the darkened closet. The door shut behind them and the two co-captains stood there uneasily in the semi-darkness. After about thirty seconds, Abraham couldn't take the silence any longer and had to say something.

"It's OK, we don't have to do any…"

Unexpectedly, Tobias tilted his head down and leaned forward, silencing Abraham with a big, open-mouthed kiss. Abraham was stunned to say the least, but once he got over the initial shock he realized that he was actually enjoying the kiss. It wasn't how he'd imagined his first proper kiss, but considering it was with a drunk straight guy who happened to be his friend and whose girlfriend was sitting just outside, it wasn't half bad. Their tongues circled each other slowly at first, then far more passionately. Abraham could taste the yeasty remnants of the beer Tobias had been drinking but it wasn't unpleasant and he found himself eagerly giving into the kiss. His natural instincts came to the fore and he drew Tobias in even tighter, although part of him desperately wished it were Lincoln in his arms instead. His hands moved down and firmly cupped Tobias' plump buttocks through the sarong, which drew a grunt of appreciation from the Sea God.

As they kissed, their bodies pressed harder into one another and Abraham could soon feel Tobias' manhood rapidly hardening against him, which was being reciprocated in his own pants. He enjoyed the rough sensation of Tobias' stubble rubbing against his face as they kissed. Abraham's brain was abuzz with questions.

What if he wants to do more? That monster of his will probably kill me! Is this how I want to lose my virginity?

Suddenly, there was a loud banging on the door, causing them to break apart.

"Time's up, boys!" came Lydia's somewhat garbled voice through the door.

Ten minutes already?

"You're a pretty good kisser, Abe," murmured Tobias.

"Thanks, you too."

They opened the door and returned to the excited cheers of the group, especially after they saw Tobias' very obvious erection straining under the thin material of the sarong. Lydia, however, seemed far less impressed. Abraham looked over to Topher who was smirking and gave him a wink.

"Whose turn is it?" squealed Penny.

"Topher's I think," answered Jonas.

Topher grasped the phone in his hand and sent it twirling around the center of the bed. The next one to be chosen was Austin, who, to everyone's great amusement, was then forced to spank Topher in front of the group – not that either participant seemed to mind in the slightest. Even Abraham had relaxed enough to enjoy the naughtiness of their game. The next several spins saw a few more acts of public affection and also sent various couples to the closet, all of which exited far more disheveled than they'd entered. By this point, the effects of the alcohol were starting to wear off and Abraham was beginning to doubt that he'd have the chance to be with Lincoln.

As luck would have it, the very next turn saw Lincoln set the phone in motion.

Please let it be with me. Please let it be with me.

Sadly, it was with a sense of crushing disappointment that Abraham witnessed the arrow glide straight past him and settle just to his right on Penny, with the instruction of five minutes of private time.

"OMG! My turn again!" screamed Penny, not even attempting to disguise her delight.

Even in his state of disillusionment, Abraham couldn't help but notice the slight look of annoyance that crossed over Jonas' face, presumably in reaction to Penny's grand enthusiasm for the game. Abraham felt annoyed as well but then rebuked himself.

He's not my boyfriend. Besides I just kissed Tobias, what right do I have to get upset? Grow up!

Not too long later, Penny and Lincoln exited the closet, both looking rather content, which made Abraham's heart twinge and his stomach feel unsettled – admittedly that could have been from the multiple Blue Zombies swishing about inside of it. The game went on for another few rounds but Abraham was no longer in the mood for such fun.

He motioned to Topher that he was leaving and got up to go.

"You, OK?" mouthed Topher.

Abraham gave him a curt nod in return and wandered from the room without saying goodbye. As he reached the doorway, Abraham turned to look back at Lincoln who was chatting animatedly with Lydia.

He doesn't even notice I'm going.

The thought began to depress him, so Abraham beat a hasty retreat, heading downstairs and out into the chilly autumn's night. Fortunately, his house was only a few blocks away, so, after a brief walk home, Abraham was soon cozily wrapped up in bed.

As he drifted off to sleep, Abraham replayed the evening's events over and over again. His happiness and excitement over his experience with Tobias were tempered by his longing for Lincoln.

Do I have a chance with him? Should I man up and just ask him out? I'm such a pussy!

* * *

Two Saturdays later, Abraham and Lincoln were sitting side by side at his desk. The window was open and a pleasant autumn breeze gently billowed the curtains, keeping the air in the room fresh. It was their third tutoring session and Abraham was happy with Lincoln's progress in such a short time.

They were seated so near to one another that Abraham felt the warmth emanating from Lincoln's toned arm. Even though Abraham was in professional teacher mode, he still had to occasionally remind himself to concentrate on the work and not the Adonis beside him. Not an easy task given their close proximity, as it also meant that Abraham could smell the thoroughly intoxicating natural musk of his student – a heady combination of pheromones and perspiration.

"So, the cells use the *monomers* released from breaking down *polymers* to construct new polymer molecules," recited Lincoln.

"Yes, that's right."

"Or they can degrade the monomers even more into simple waste products."

"Bonus point if you can name two of the potential waste products," declared Abraham in the style of an excitable game show host.

"Umm…lactic acid and…umm…carbon dioxide?"

"Perfect!" Abraham beamed with pleasure. "You're really getting a handle on it."

"Well, it's all thanks to my teacher."

"Thanks, but you've done the work."

"Yes, Sir. But I can't tell ya how much I appreciate your help and…"

Lincoln stopped mid-sentence; their faces were barely an inch apart. Abraham was intoxicated by Lincoln's honey-scented breath – due to the Double Bees he always seemed to be sucking on. All Abraham could focus on was Lincoln's plump, pinkish-brown lips and how much he wanted to taste them. His heart was racing inside his chest as Lincoln slowly moved his head forward towards him. They were a mere second away from locking lips when the door was suddenly flung open causing the boys to rush back apart. It was Abraham's sister, Megan, a tiny, thirteen-year-old menace with a mouth-full of bright-pink braces and a spray of pimples on her forehead – artfully concealed behind her light-brown bangs.

"Mom wants to know if Lincoln is staying for dinner," stated Megan in a thoroughly bored manner.

"Jesus, Megan! Can't you knock! Get out. Now!"

Megan flinched at her brother's uncharacteristic harsh timbre. She turned away from the boys, her face full of teenage fury, and yelled down the hallway.

"MOM! Abe's being mean to me!"

Her whiny tone of voice only served to aggravate Abraham further, so he jumped up from his chair and pushed her firmly out of his room, closing the door with a resounding thud behind her.

"I'm so sorry about that. She's always busting in...umm, so, did you want to stay for dinner?"

"No, I can't unfortunately. I already have plans, but thank ya kindly for the offer."

"Oh, sure no problem."

The disappointment was evident in Abraham's voice, despite his efforts to hide how he was feeling.

"I should get going. Thanks for today."

"That's fine; it's my job, after all."

"I hope we can pick up where we left off next time, Beau."

"Sure, of course."

Does he mean the study or the kiss?

He escorted Lincoln downstairs and out of the house. On his way back to his room, Abraham encountered Megan in the hallway.

"Don't ever do that again!" growled Abraham, in the menacing tone normally found between fighting siblings.

"Why? Did I interrupt something?" teased Megan.

"That's...I don't...it doesn't matter. My room is private. OK?"

"Whatever!"

They both stomped off to their rooms and banged the doors firmly behind them.

Why did she have to come in? I can't believe we almost kissed! Hopefully, next time.

* * *

Abraham had just finished his fifth training session for the week and was absolutely exhausted. The rest of the squad had gone home half an hour beforehand but he'd wanted to really push himself. Normally, Tobias would've stayed behind as well, as they both liked to encourage each other with their training, but he'd had a family dinner to get to. Happily, things hadn't changed between the co-captains after their steamy kiss in the closet, with the only reference to their encounter being the occasional sly smile exchanged between the pair. Even Tobias' girlfriend, Lydia, had stopped being standoffish a few days afterwards, obviously choosing to pretend that it hadn't taken place at all.

The change rooms were empty but Abraham could hear a few of the showers running. He was very much looking forward to the weekend and his next tutoring session with Lincoln. They had seen each other in class during the week and while their behavior had been friendly enough, Abraham couldn't wait to be alone with him again.

With his thoughts full of what might happen that coming Saturday, Abraham slowly stripped off his Speedos, wrapped a large, blue towel around himself and wearily padded along to the group shower area. Abraham turned the corner of the tiled area and stopped dead in his tracks. There, against the far wall, were a couple of naked guys kissing under the showers. It wasn't the unexpected erotic display, however, that had caused him to stop, as it certainly wasn't the first time he'd seen such things in the school showers. Nor, was it the fact that one of the guys was Jonas, as his burgeoning bisexuality was something of an open secret amongst the senior class. In fact, he'd hooked up with quite a few guys during his intermittent breaks with Penny, which appeared to be the case today. Rather, what had shocked Abraham was the identity of the other guy in the passionate tryst.

Lincoln!

If Abraham hadn't been so emotionally invested in Lincoln, he would have found the whole scene unquestionably hot. Jonas looked every inch the All-American-Boy, with tousled blonde hair, clear-blue eyes and a solid athletic build, without an ounce of fat to be seen; all of which contrasted beautifully against Lincoln's mocha-colored skin and strong, dark features.

How could he do this to me?

Lincoln broke away from the kiss and glanced over to the entrance and saw Abraham. His face suddenly awash with emotion, most prominently surprise and a helping of guilt.

"Abe?" said Lincoln.

Jonas also looked over towards Abraham but his visage held a much more mischievous regard. His fatigue forgotten, Abraham didn't say a word and simply rushed out of the shower area and almost ran back to his locker. He hurriedly threw on his clothes and headed out the door before either of the guys made it out of the showers. As he left he heard Lincoln calling out to him again.

"Abe, wait!"

But he wasn't in the mood for whatever Lincoln had to say. He rushed to the bus stop out the front of the school and jumped on the first one that arrived. It wasn't his usual bus, and he'd have to walk a few more blocks at the other end, but he desperately wanted to be as far away as possible from what he'd just witnessed. Abraham wanted to forget all about it but his mind wouldn't stop whirring all the way home.

Why did I think he'd ever want me? I'm such an idiot! He's so out of my league. I guess he was just toying with me.

* * *

The following day, Abraham was perched on a stool in the biology lab, waiting for the class to begin and still feeling slightly miserable…and quite sorry for himself. Lincoln hadn't yet arrived and part of him hoped that he wouldn't come. Abraham dreaded seeing him again after what he'd encountered in the showers. In an effort to take his mind off of Lincoln, Abraham stared intently at his textbook, doing the reading for the following topic. He became so engrossed that he didn't even notice that Lincoln had sat down beside him.

"Abe. Why didn't ya come back when I called?" inquired Lincoln softly.

Abraham jumped at the unexpected voice, and then blushed furiously at his foolishness. Without looking at his lab partner, Abraham attempted to justify his actions.

"I...I didn't want to...I'm sorry that I interrupted you."

"Ya didn't interrupt anything."

There was a firmness to Lincoln's voice that made Abraham look up and turn to him.

"Really?" Abraham tried to stop himself from sounding too overtly interested in Lincoln's declaration. "I mean...it's none of my concern."

"Are ya upset with me, Beau?"

"No...why would I be? You were making out with Jonas. It's not my business."

"He kissed me."

"Well you seemed to be kissing him back." Abraham shot back, his voice brimming with anger.

"So, ya *are* jealous, Beau!" teased Lincoln.

Realizing that he'd betrayed his feelings, Abraham desperately tried to backpedal.

"No...why would I...I don't care...and why do you keep calling me that?"

"Because you're beautiful."

There was such sincerity to Lincoln's simple statement, and in his eyes, that Abraham was shocked into silence.

He really thinks I'm beautiful?

"Sure Jonas is pretty damn hot, but he's not who I'm interested in," continued Lincoln, a sly smile dancing on his lips.

"Oh?"

Does he mean?

"In case ya were wondering, it's *you!*"

Abraham was completely flabbergasted and didn't know how to respond. He had dreamed about this moment enough times but never thought it would come true. Fighting an almost overwhelming urge to stand up on the desk and shout about his happiness, Abraham settled for sitting on his stool and grinning like an idiot instead.

"Would ya do me the honor of accompanying me to the movies tomorrow night, kind sir?" requested Lincoln, southern charm exuding from every pore.

"OK," Abraham replied timidly, the huge grin still plastered across his face.

"Well, that was easy."

They were interrupted in their conversation by an unmistakably irritated voice booming from the front of the classroom.

"Gentlemen, if you're quite finished would you mind terribly if we started today's lesson?"

"Sorry, Mrs. Mears," said the boys in unison.

Despite the chastening, Abraham couldn't wipe the wide smile off of his face, which stayed firmly in place for the rest of the day. It was doubtful that anything short of an apocalypse could have removed it.

I have a date!

* * *

Abraham was locked in a state of nervous excitement that only continued to build as the day wore on but he wouldn't have wanted it any other way. Every time he thought about the upcoming date his heart swelled, and to be honest, so did his crotch. It wasn't until they were actually sitting in the cinema together the following evening, however, that Abraham could slowly start to relax and enjoy the experience without over analyzing everything – well not excessively at any rate.

Earlier that day, Lincoln had come over for his usual tutoring session, although they had spent most of the time smiling at each other and not really concentrating on the task at hand. When he'd gone, Abraham had immediately summoned Topher over from next door to help him prepare. The pair spent the next few hours painstakingly choosing an outfit for the date and Abraham's bedroom floor was soon littered with rejects. Eventually, they settled on a simple pair of light-gray pants and a green shirt that worked well with his hair and light coloring.

"Are you sure I look, OK?" fretted Abraham.

"You look absolutely fuckable!" exclaimed Topher. "If I didn't have Eli, I'd already have pinned you to the bed myself."

"Ha! Thanks." Abraham stood preening in front of the mirror. "But what I'll do if he wants to fuck me tonight?"

It was a question he'd posed several times in the past hour and Topher patiently answered as he had the previous times.

"He's a good guy and I'm sure he won't pressure you. Stop stressing and just have fun."

Just then Abraham's phone buzzed with a text from Lincoln.

"He'll be here in five minutes!" exclaimed Abraham, practically buzzing with excitement.

"That's my cue to head off. Call me as soon as you get home. I want to hear every last disgusting detail."

Abraham saw Topher out but then lingered by the front door. His parents were upstairs and he wanted to be able to rush out as soon as he heard Lincoln's jeep and not have to explain where he was going, what he was doing or with whom.

I'm not a little boy any more. They don't need to know everything.

Right at the appointed time, Lincoln pulled up out the front and Abraham barely restrained himself from running towards the freshly washed, Royal-blue Jeep. Lincoln opened the passenger door from the inside and greeted Abraham with his customary dazzlingly white smile. He was dressed in dark-blue jeans, a tight, white t-shirt and a fitted black jacket, all of which only served to enhance his natural beauty.

"Damn, Beau, ya look fine!"

"Thanks," said Abraham blushing. "You too."

They chatted amiably on the journey to the city and it seemed to Abraham that they'd reached their destination in only a matter of moments. Not long afterwards, he and Lincoln were seated together in the middle section of the Rex cinema, with a large box of buttery popcorn between them, watching the advertisements play before the main feature – Wait Until Dark. Abraham wasn't a huge fan of old films but he'd eagerly agreed when Lincoln had suggested it. To be frank, a small part of Abraham was genuinely worried that if he weren't amenable to everything then Lincoln would realize that he'd made a terrible mistake and change his mind.

Besides it's Audrey Hepburn, it'll be a fun romance.

To his great surprise, the film wasn't at all what Abraham had thought. Instead of the fun romp he'd been expecting, it was an edge-of-the-seat thriller. The one advantage was that he'd clung onto Lincoln's delightfully muscular arm quite early on and hadn't let go. Judging by the contented smile on Lincoln's face, this may have been his plan all along.

After the film, at Lincoln's suggestion, they headed to a nearby café – One Happy Piggy – to continue their date. They sat on the terrace under one of the large, silver space heaters and began to peruse the menu.

"I love this place. Ya really gotta try the sweet potatoes with bacon, they're absolutely divine."

"Hey Angelboy! Good to see you again. And who's this handsome young buck?" asked the buxom middle-aged waitress, whose Southern drawl matched Lincoln's.

She seems awfully familiar with her customers.

"Abe this is my Aunt Gloria and the owner of this fine establishment."

"Pleased to meet you," said Abraham giving Gloria a shy smile.

He wasn't expecting to meet Lincoln's family on the first date and was feeling fairly intimidated.

"Why aren't ya just the sweetest thing? I'm gonna fix you boys something special."

"Could we get some of those delicious sweet potatoes, Ma'am?" inquired Lincoln, flashing his winning smile.

"Of course, sugar. Anything for my favorite nephew. It'll be ready in a jiffy."

And with that she sashayed away off to the kitchen, a sassy confidence radiating from every step.

"So your Aunt moved out here with your family?"

"Naw, she's been living up North for about twenty years. She's been telling my momma how great Port Davinica is for years. So, when my dad ran away with his secretary my momma decided we all needed a fresh start."

Despite Lincoln's light attitude, Abraham could sense a degree of sadness behind his words.

"I'm so sorry. I didn't realize."

"It's fine. I don't really talk about it. My dad and I weren't really close, and his leaving was such a cliché, so I don't feel like I lost anything. And anyway, if we hadn't moved I'd never had met ya and that would have been a damn shame."

Abraham blushed at the compliment. He adored that Lincoln was opening up to him and their connection felt even stronger as the evening wore on. As promised, the sweet potatoes were indeed scrumptious, as was the rest of the food they'd wolfed down. Abraham had tried to pay but his offer had been thoroughly rejected by both Lincoln and Gloria, the latter appeared almost insulted by the notion.

After they'd bid Gloria a fond farewell, Lincoln began the drive to take Abraham back home. All too soon, they pulled up out the front of Abraham's place.

"Thanks for a great evening. I really enjoyed myself," declared Abraham.

"Me too, Beau," agreed Lincoln softly.

Lincoln moved forward and his full lips lightly grazed Abraham's. Their kiss started off delicately but quickly became more passionate, with the obvious hunger between them coming to the fore.

This is so much better than kissing Tobias.

As they kissed, Abraham ran his hands through the tightly wound curls of Lincoln's cropped hair, he loved the thick feel of it, so very different from the silkiness of his own. The crotch of Abraham's pants became rather tight as his erection tried to escape its confinement. Their hands grabbed at one another with Lincoln's moving ever downwards, closer and closer to Abraham's groin. As excited as he was, Abraham was also nervous and worried about his total lack of experience, which is probably why he suddenly blurted out.

"I'm a virgin!"

What did I just say? Am I completely insane? Shut up, shut up, shut up!

Lincoln sat back slightly with a perplexed expression plastered on his face.

"What did ya say?" Lincoln asked gently.

I've fucked up everything! I'm such an idiot!

"I'm a virgin. Look I'm really sorry to spring it on you but I just thought you should know before we got too far along."

A wave of shame swept over Abraham, who was positive that he'd just ruined any chance of their continued dating. He looked away from Lincoln, expecting to be turfed out of the jeep at any moment.

"Ah, OK...I was one too once ya know." Lincoln said in an obvious attempt to break the tension. "It's really not a big deal."

"Yeah, I'm just kinda embarrassed about it."

"It's fine. I haven't been with that many guys myself and I'm not expecting anything of ya." Lincoln took Abraham by the hand and looked sweetly into his eyes. "We don't have to do anything ya don't wanna do, I promise. Of course, I find ya attractive and would love to mess around but you're an amazing guy regardless."

It was the perfect response. Abraham's face flushed pink with the compliment but he was certain that he'd destroyed the mood nevertheless.

"Thanks for a great evening." Abraham readjusted his shirt, which had come astray during their embrace. "I should probably get going."

"OK, Beau. See ya Monday."

"Can't wait."

He gave Lincoln a quick kiss goodbye and fled inside.

Why did I tell him that??? But he said he's still keen. He was probably just being polite. I'm a mess!

* * *

"Why the *hell* did you tell him that?" demanded Topher, echoing Abraham's own thoughts, exasperation clearly showing in his voice. "Get over here now!"

True to his word, Abraham had called Topher as soon as he got home and delivered a highly emotional recounting of the evening's events.

"Look it's late; we can chat about it tomorrow."

"Yeah but you're probably just going to stew about it all night anyway," countered Topher. "Just come over and we'll have a sleep over like we used to and gossip about boys...or just about the one in particular."

"Your parents won't mind?"

"Please! You know they think of you as practically another son."

Abraham knew that it was a much better idea than staying at home and driving himself crazy.

"Alright, I'll be over in a sec."

He quickly packed an overnight bag and headed next door. Five minutes later, Abraham was sitting on Topher's bed looking expectantly at his best friend for answers.

"I can't believe you blurted it out like that. What were you thinking?"

"I don't know!" Abraham sighed miserably. "I was thinking too much I guess. Maybe 'cause I was so nervous and I was worried things might go too far."

"He was hardly going to fuck you right in front of your house," scoffed Topher.

"I know…but it just all seemed to happening so fast."

"It sounds like he was OK with it, at least."

Abraham was far from persuaded and desperately wanted to stop the doubts whirring about his brain.

"ERGHH! Why did I have to be so stupid and honest?"

"Abe, calm down. I think you're worrying over nothing."

"But I really like him and I think I fucked it all up."

Abraham could hear the teenage whine coming into his voice and hated himself for it.

I sound like Megan!

"Do I need to slap you?" demanded Topher.

Even though Topher's face was a picture of seriousness, Abraham knew that he was joking and only trying to snap him out of the freefall of uncertainty. He appreciated the effort and tried his very best to quell his misgivings over the end of the date.

"Nah…you'd probably like it too much."

"True." Topher smirked. "You know, there's nothing wrong with being a virgin."

"Easy for you to say. You've got Eli…*and* you guys fuck like rabbits on ecstasy."

"Yeah we do." The pride in his voice was unmistakable. "But that's only been this past year and before that I was in exactly the same place as you. It's OK to be nervous and want to wait until it's the right guy. I got lucky finding Eli and I'm sure it'll be the same for you and Lincoln."

"I know…but…what if he wants someone more *experienced*."

"I'm sure Lincoln is fine with it, like he said. He doesn't seem the type to play games."

"Maybe."

Abraham still wasn't completely convinced and fiddled anxiously with the corner of one of Topher's pillows. Fortunately, Topher wasn't one to give up without a fight.

"Besides if he is the *right* guy, he'll wait until you're ready. You're awesome and if he doesn't respect that then he doesn't deserve you."

"I guess."

"And trust me when you do end up going all the way you'll never want to stop."

"Well…what we did already felt *so* amazing! If we'd been in a bed I'm not sure I would've been able to stop," admitted Abraham, his eyes sparkling with mischief.

"Just think, when you do finally pop that prize cherry you won't have to jack off anywhere near as much. I mean I'd happily do it for you but Eli would probably object...or at least want to watch."

"Thanks, good to know." Abraham rolled his eyes and poked out his tongue. "You're such a comfort."

"I know." Topher responded with a smug grin.

The pair hugged and for the first time since his admission to Lincoln, Abraham had the sense that things would work out. They broke apart and Abraham switched topics to their looming college applications – another reason to stress and something that would definitely keep them both preoccupied for quite some time. They stayed up half the night discussing their future plans, before eventually succumbing to sleep. The lads slumbered happily curled up together, platonically, in Topher's exceedingly comfortable bed, which was how Mrs. Walker found them the following morning when she came in to let them know breakfast was ready.

* * *

Lincoln wasn't at school the following Monday, or the Tuesday for that matter, and Abraham was beginning to get worried. He hadn't called Lincoln since Saturday, as he hadn't wanted to come across as needy or desperate but was beginning to regret his decision.

Maybe he's really sick? And I didn't even call him! Now he definitely won't bother with my pathetic sexless self.

Abraham vowed that if he didn't see Lincoln on the Wednesday he would call or maybe even go over to his house to see he was still alive. Happily, Abraham was saved from such drastic action when he got to biology to find a tired-looking

Lincoln already seated at their desk. Relief flooded into his body as he sat down beside his lab partner.

"Hi, are you OK?" asked Abraham, his worry evident.

"Yeah, just had a big ol' tummy bug, my momma had it too, but I'm much better now. I'm just glad that I didn't make ya sick after we kissed."

"I'm glad…I mean, not that you were sick but that you're better."

Lincoln laughed lightheartedly at Abraham's awkwardness. He laid his hand on top of Abraham's in a tender gesture of reassurance.

"I knew what ya meant, Beau."

"I'm sorry I didn't call you after the date," apologized Abraham guiltily.

"Don't worry; I wasn't really in the mood to talk to anyone. And ya ain't getting rid of me that easily."

"So…you still want to go out with me, even though I'm a…"

"Of course, Beau. That's not why I want to date ya…well not the only reason. You're damn cute, and smart, and I like ya."

Abraham felt himself blushing and was sure that his face was a mask of telltale red.

"I like you too."

"As soon as I'm all better, you and I are going out again, Mister."

"Yes, Sir."

He really likes me!

"That's what I like to hear."

The pair sat staring at one another, with goofy grins on their faces, holding hands and completely unaware of the world around them. Undoubtedly, they could have stayed like this for the rest of the day but their bubble of happiness was suddenly pierced by a sharp voice from up the front of the classroom.

"Gentlemen, I do realize that you find each other infinitely more interesting than the genetic properties of chimpanzees but you could at least pay me the courtesy of pretending to listen when I'm speaking."

There was a great deal of tittering and giggling amongst their classmates and the boys quickly turned their attentions to the front.

"Yes, Mrs. Mears," said Abraham.

"Sorry, Mrs. Mears," added Lincoln.

Even though Abraham felt thoroughly chastised, he couldn't help repeatedly glancing at Lincoln who was doing the same in return. Every time their eyes caught one another Abraham was filled with a joy that made his face beam.

* * *

The weather had turned decidedly wintry and the city was being covered in a pristine sheet of fresh, white snow on a regular basis. The Christmas break was fast approaching and Abraham was the happiest he'd ever been in his short life. He and Lincoln had been officially dating for a little over a month and everything felt very right with the world. Each time their dates had ended with fierce session of heavy petting in Lincoln's jeep, but their hands tended to stay above the clothing – mostly. Not to say there wasn't much rubbing and groping though said clothes.

Abraham was happy with what they had but he knew that things would naturally progress at some point – men have needs, after all, and his self-pleasuring wasn't going to suffice indefinitely. Part of Abraham was desperate to go all the way with his new boyfriend but he was still hesitant. It wasn't that he didn't trust Lincoln's intentions. Rather, Abraham just wanted to wait until they'd been together a little longer before taking such a big step...although his crotch was becoming increasingly insistent on the matter.

For his part, Lincoln had been wonderfully understanding and a perfect gentleman, not putting any pressure on Abraham. He had let Abraham take the lead in their encounters, even though it was abundantly clear that he'd be naked and ready to go in an instant, once given the go-ahead.

The air was crisp and the boys were currently gliding around the ice rink in front of the Town Hall, surrounded by a great many similarly inclined individuals wrapped up in their winter finery. The two held hands as they skated around the rink, partly for support but also because they quite liked touching one another whenever possible. Even though he still wasn't out to the world at large, Abraham wasn't really concerned about being seen by people he knew. Every time he was with Lincoln he felt safe and secure and entirely unconcerned by the rest of the world. Abraham was without a doubt in the first throes of love – as was Lincoln, given the reciprocating look of adoration in his eyes whenever they were together. The depth of Abraham's feelings towards Lincoln easily eclipsed those he'd possessed for his former crushes – his heart was virgin no more.

Of course, it was only a matter of time before he was brought crashing back into reality – literally. They were headed towards the benches at the side when they were knocked sideways by a full-figured lady of a certain age.

"Oh, I'm so sorry, I'm terrible at this…Abraham Chadwick is that you?" asked the woman.

Abraham realized that their inadvertent attacker was his dentist, Dr. Amanda Cohen; a jolly lady in her late fifties, with a kindly disposition, wide brown eyes and wild chestnut curls streaked silver with age.

"Dr. Cohen? What are you doing here?" demanded Abraham, shocked by the unexpected meeting.

"Failing miserably, I'm afraid. I haven't skated for years and my daughter thought I should give it a whirl. She's twirling about the rink here somewhere. Oh dear, I hope I haven't hurt you or your handsome young companion."

Abraham looked to Lincoln, who smiled back and showed no sign of injury.

"Nah, I think we're all good." Suddenly, remembering his manners, Abraham began to introduce everyone. "Dr. Cohen this is Lincoln, my…friend."

Abraham saw the unmistakable look of hurt and disappointment in Lincoln's eyes and felt instantly ashamed that he hadn't said 'boyfriend.'

Why must I ruin everything!

"Lovely to meet you, young man. And good to see you too, Abraham. Well, I must go and get off the ice before I go and maim anyone else. See you at your next check up!"

After she'd skated off, or rather wobbled precariously toward the exit, Abraham turned to Lincoln and began to apologize.

"I'm sorry, Linc. It's just that she sees my whole family and I didn't feel right telling her you were my boyfriend before I'd even told my family."

"Will that be any time soon?" asked Lincoln politely, although there was a certain hard edge to his voice.

Guilt flooded into Abraham's heart. Not only was he denying Lincoln sex, now Abraham was denying his very existence.

"I...I hadn't really planned on when." Abraham hastily continued after seeing a darkening look on Lincoln's face. "But I clearly should. I'm not ashamed of you, or me, but I was kinda waiting for the right time."

"I understand that it's hard but I already came out of the closet and I don't wanna have to go back in."

Abraham understood well Lincoln's point of view and was annoyed at himself for not addressing the situation earlier.

I need to fix this.

"I know, I know. I'm sorry if I made you upset. You're so important to me."

"I feel the same way about ya, Beau."

"I promise, I'll do it soon," reassured Abraham.

"That's all I ask."

Abraham took Lincoln's hand and together they headed to the benches to take off their skates. The topic of his coming out wasn't discussed on their car ride home but it was pretty much all that Abraham could think about.

I need to tell them soon. Lincoln is too important to risk losing over this.

* * *

Following the incident at the ice rink, Abraham had turned to Topher for advice about how to best break the news to his family.

"Do it somewhere private where you feel comfortable and you have time to talk about it with them afterwards. But honestly, your parents are cool. I'm sure they'll be totally fine," counseled Topher.

"I guess you're right. And I need to do it for myself and for Lincoln."

"That you do. Besides, you can always come here if it goes badly." Topher hastened to add. "Which it won't!"

Abraham had no real fear that they'd react poorly, as his parents had been the ones to teach him from an early age to be accepting and open to other people's differences. And it was hardly as if Abraham were the first pink sheep of the family. Indeed, they'd all happily attended the wedding of his father's youngest sister, Aunt Holly, to her wife, Victoria, the year before.

A few days later, Abraham and his family were seated around the table, midway through their habitual Sunday roast dinner. Seated together, there was no mistaking the family connection. Abraham had inherited his auburn hair from his mother and his father's clear blue eyes and lean build. Both his parents were in their early forties but still retained a youthful air, even though his father's black hair was beginning to gray at the temples. His mother, Sheila, was naturally curvy and shared her emerald-green eyes with Abraham's sister Megan.

"Mom, Dad...I have something I wanted to talk to you about."

"What is it, Nemo?" asked Abraham's father, Burt.

It has been his father's nickname for him ever since Abraham could remember, partly due to his obsession with the film when he was a child and his subsequent passion for swimming.

"I have something to tell you." Abraham's pulse was racing and his mouth suddenly felt dry and scratchy. Summoning all of his inner courage, Abraham took a deep breath and let out the secret he'd been keeping for as long as he could remember. "I'm...I'm gay."

"Erghh, so *not* a surprise," teased Megan, rolling here eyes melodramatically.

"Megan!" scolded Sheila.

"Whaaat? I was only saying what we're all think..."

"Go to your room now, missy!

"But, Mom..."

"No, I don't want to hear it. Go to your room until you can act like the polite young lady that I thought we raised."

Megan stomped out of the room and up the stairs, which was shortly followed by the loud slamming of a door.

Abraham's parents exchanged a look of quiet exasperation and turned their attentions back to their son.

"I'm sorry about that, honey." Sheila said in her most motherly tone. "Your sister obviously forgot her manners today."

"It's OK. She's right."

"That's neither here nor there dear. Megan knows better than to belittle people."

"We understand that this is difficult for you, Nemo, but you know that we love you no matter what. You're our son," reassured Burt.

"You can always come to us," added Sheila.

"Thanks. Yeah I know."

There was an awkward silence as Abraham wasn't sure what to say. He'd only really planned the announcement. His mother, however, seemed to know exactly where to take the conversation.

"Is there anyone special in your life, Abe?" inquired Sheila tentatively.

"Yeah, actually there is," admitted Abraham with a shy smile.

Of course, she wants to know everything!

"Is it Lincoln?"

"Yes…he's my boyfriend."

"I knew it…I told you, Burt," exclaimed Sheila, a look of self-satisfaction plastered upon her face.

Guess I haven't been as inconspicuous as I thought.

"Yes, Sheila."

His father gave Abraham a conspiratorial wink and a knowing smile.

"So, I hope you're being careful, dear."

"MOM!"

"We would say the same to your sister…when she is allowed to start dating."

"It's embarrassing." Abraham complained while squirming uncomfortably in his chair.

"Yes, Abe, but it is important," added Burt.

"We're not even doing that!" exclaimed Abraham, truly mortified.

"Well at least we don't have to worry about any teenage pregnancies," remarked his father, lightheartedly

"I wish I hadn't said anything," muttered Abraham.

"Don't be like that, Nemo. We're glad that you felt comfortable telling us. Isn't that right, Sheila?"

"Yes, of course. But you really must invite him around for dinner."

"Yes, we need to get to know this young man and see if he's good enough for our son," said Burt, in a show of mock seriousness.

"You've already met him. Please don't make a big deal about it."

"Nonsense, if he's special to you, then he's special to us," proclaimed Sheila.

"Fine, can we please stop talking about it?"

As embarrassed as he was, Abraham was also pleased that his family had been so accepting – even if his kid sister had been a little brat about it. He felt a new sense of lightness about being completely honest – one less teenage stress at least. Thankfully, the talk then turned to Abraham's upcoming swim meet and his training.

Later that evening, Abraham was up in his room finishing off the reading for the following day's history class, when there was a light tapping on the door.

"Yes?"

"It's me…can I come in?" Megan's timid voice came through the door.

Abraham huffed and did hid best to suppress his irritability at his sister, although it was hard to fight years of sibling resentment.

"I don't know. Are you still being a little monster?"

"Abe!"

"Alright! Come in."

Megan opened the door and sheepishly entered. The last time Abraham had seen her look so guilty was when she'd been caught trying to sneak out to a high school party she'd been expressly forbidden from attending.

"What do you want?" asked Abraham gruffly.

"Look, I'm sorry about what I said. I think it's great that you're gay and that you have a boyfriend."

Does everyone know?

"How did you know that I have a…"

"Well my bedroom does face the front and you and Lincoln always take forever to say goodbye. I mean it's kinda gross…"

"Meg!"

Abraham was discomfited and annoyed that his privacy had been violated, although it was becoming increasingly apparent that he hadn't been particularly discreet.

"Sorry…so anyway, do you forgive me?"

"Yeah, I guess."

"Great! Now can you go tell Mom and Dad so I'm not in trouble any more? Pleeease?"

"Ergggh, fine."

"You're the best!"

She's so annoying!

Despite his irritation, Abraham couldn't help but smile as he watched her practically skip away down the hallway to her room. She'd always be his baby sister, no matter how bratty she acted.

* * *

Abraham had put off the official family dinner with Lincoln until after the Christmas festivities had passed, as he wanted to delay the possibility of his parents embarrassing him for as long as possible. He'd made them promise not to show any of his baby photos or bring up any cringe-worthy stories from his childhood. In regards to his sister, Abraham had reluctantly bribed her into good behavior with the pledge to lobby their parents to let her go the One Direction concert with her friends the following month.

The boys had spent Christmas Day itself with their respective families, although they'd met up Christmas Eve and exchanged small tokens of their affection – a sonic screwdriver for Lincoln and a Captain Reynolds action figure for Abraham.

The first Sunday night of the New Year saw the Chadwick family seated at their dining room table with their guest of honor seated right beside Abraham. Under the table their legs were pushed up against one another, rubbing gently together.

Lincoln had commenced with his full-on charm offensive from the moment he walked in the door, presenting a large bouquet of lilacs to Abraham's mother – her favorite – and a small box of Turkish Delight for Abraham's father – his favorite. He'd done his homework well. To secure the deal, Lincoln had even brought a homemade peach-pecan cobbler for dessert – Abraham couldn't have been prouder.

"It's so good of y'all to invite me," said Lincoln graciously, his words practically coated with honey. "I can see where Abe gets his beautiful hair from, Ma'am."

"Why aren't you just a charming young man? And please, call me Sheila," gushed Abraham's mother.

Abraham was a little disturbed to see that his mother seemed to be almost flustered by Lincoln's compliments.

Is she flirting with my boyfriend?

Regardless, Abraham was pleased to see that his parents had been won over almost immediately by the handsome, and thoroughly polite, Southern boy. Even Megan seemed to have dropped her usual level of snarky adolescence for the meal...as much as was humanly possible.

"So, how do you like living up North, Lincoln?" asked Abraham's father.

"Oh, it's different but I do like it here, Sir. There're so many special things I've discovered."

Lincoln turned and smiled at Abraham, who in turn reddened and smiled widely.

God, he's perfect!

"That's good to hear and please no more of this Sir and Ma'am. We don't stand on ceremony here. Burt will do just fine."

"Yes, Si...Burt. Thank ya kindly. These carrots are amazing...Sheila." Lincoln was clearly having a little difficulty with addressing elders so informally. "Just like my granny's back home."

"Why, thank you, dear."

"What's it like to be on the cheer squad?" demanded Megan. "Is it a lot of training? I was thinking of going for tryouts next semester."

"Were you just?" asked Burt, it was apparently the first he'd heard of it.

"Well you're always telling me I should do sports and stuff. Plus, the cheerleaders get to date all the footballers."

"Or the swim captain," added Lincoln cheekily.

Abraham gave his boyfriend a playful tap on the arm and a look of mock disapproval.

"I'm not so sure that's..." began Burt, his overprotective fathering instincts obviously coming to the fore.

"Oh, Burt. This isn't the time, not in front of company," scolded Sheila lightly.

"Don't mind me," said Lincoln. "It's just me and my momma at home and I miss our family back in New Orleans. I think you'd make a fine cheerleader, Megan, but it's a lot of hard work and takes up a lot of your time. And ya have to take care not to get injured."

Megan now looked a little unsure of her plans and Abraham's parents seemed pleased at his diffusing of the situation.

By the end of the meal, Abraham was even more enamored with Lincoln – if such a thing was possible – and couldn't wait to show his appreciation on their next date. He was starting to feel that perhaps he was ready to take things further with Lincoln – perhaps not quite all the way but a fair way along the path to pleasure, at any rate.

* * *

A few evenings later Abraham and Lincoln were in the car park of The Head – a popular parking spot for frisky couples, on a bluff overlooking the ocean. They were wrapped up together in the backseat of Lincoln's jeep furiously making out.

Both boys were topless, their shirts long having been discarded to the car floor, and their hands were roaming everywhere, frantically grasping and groping at one another in their passion.

Lincoln was still half-dressed in his cheerleader outfit, as they'd come straight from school after he'd finished practice, his solid erection evident through the thin material of his track pants. Meanwhile Abraham's jeans were becoming more restrictive by the second.

The air in the jeep was moist and heavy with the scent of their exertions. The contrast of the cold winter's air outside had fogged up the windows completely. Perspiration beaded on their bodies as they grappled together, their grunts and sighs reverberating in the small, enclosed space of the jeep.

Abraham was in absolute heaven. His nipples had hardened into fine points from being relentlessly tweaked and bitten by his hungry boyfriend. His cock was also showing its enthusiasm, constantly leaking precum, with a growing pool of wetness dampening the front of his jocks.

Their mouths came together once more, tongues wrestling for supremacy as their firm bodies pressed forcefully into one another. Lincoln's hand slid down and undid the top few buttons of Abraham's jeans and then hooked the waistband of his boyfriend's electric-blue CocKed underwear. His fingers crept inside, brushing over the top of the aroused member. Lincoln ran his thumb around the top of the glans, stretching the foreskin and spreading the slickness over the cockhead, causing Abraham to gasp in pleasure.

"Damn, you're delicious," whispered Lincoln after he'd brought his hand up and licked off the juice.

"Thanks," panted Abraham.

Abraham grabbed a hold of the elastic waistband of Lincoln's track pants and pulled them down to reveal scarlet-red underwear, which was bulging considerably in its efforts to try and contain a very excited monster within. Through the material, Abraham massaged along the length of the manhood, his mouth watering at the thought of tasting it. He started to pull the underwear down over the raging erection when there was a sudden rapping upon the window, accompanied by the bright powerful beam of a flashlight.

"Port Davinica P.D," came a deep, commanding voice from outside.

"Fuck! It's the police!" cursed Lincoln.

"My parents are going to kill me!" cried Abraham.

Both boys sat up in fright, frantically scrambling for their t-shirts and to do up their pants. There was another tap on the window.

"Wind down the window please, Sir."

They rearranged their clothing as best they could. Lincoln, who was closest to the window, where the policeman was standing, rolled it down slowly. There waiting outside the jeep was a strapping specimen of manhood; they could see his formidable build even with the heavy coat he was sporting. Despite his fear, Abraham could still recognize that the policeman was a very handsome man indeed. If the officer was surprised to find two young men in the backseat together he certainly didn't show it. Abraham shivered as the frigid night air rushed into the backseat.

"Is there a problem, Officer?" asked Lincoln, his voice slightly wavering.

"Good evening, gentleman. I'm Officer Ford." He flashed his gold badge at the frightened boys. "Unfortunately, I'm going to have to ask you to move your…*playtime* to a more appropriate venue."

Lincoln and Abraham simultaneously tried to vehemently deny the accusation.

"But we weren't..."

"We were only…"

"Listen guys, I was your age not too long ago and I know *exactly* what you were doing. Personally, I don't mind what you get up to but seeing this is a public place I have to ask you to move on."

"Yes, Sir," replied the boys one after the other.

"You have a good night now…and remember beds are far more comfortable!"

Officer Ford gave the boys a friendly wink and moved away. Lincoln swiftly rolled up the window again and through the haze they could see that he was now talking to the occupants of the only other car in the lot, no doubt giving them the same spiel. They clambered through the jeep to take the front seats.

"I'm so embarrassed," muttered Abraham.

"Yeah, but he was damn hot though!" declared Lincoln, obviously not too disturbed by their encounter.

"Lincoln!"

"What? I bet he liked seeing two guys going at it."

"You're incorrigible."

"What, you didn't find him sexy?" demanded Lincoln incredulously.

"That's not the point. Can we go? I don't want him to come back."

"I wouldn't mind."

"Lincoln!" rebuked Abraham.

"OK, OK. Ya know that you're the only one I want, Beau."

Abraham gave Lincoln a peck on the lips, which then progressed into a much deeper kiss. They could have easily fallen back into their previous activity if it weren't for the sound of the other car starting which made them remember the presence of the police outside.

They drove home in a companionable silence with Abraham's hand resting on Lincoln's thigh. When they pulled up in front of Abraham's house they had a very passionate goodbye, so much so that their erections came back with a vengeance. Abraham's earlier guilt at nearly getting caught was quickly overcome by his lust for his boyfriend.

As much as Abraham wanted to play so much further with Lincoln, the thought that his family was only several feet away, kept coming into his mind.

"We should…stop," gasped Abraham.

"Ya sure?" asked Lincoln, while nuzzling on Abraham's neck and rubbing his right nipple through the t-shirt.

The lads kept kissing while Abraham understandably struggled to come to a decision. Once more their clothes began to come away from their grinding bodies.

This feels so good!

"No…yes…I'm sorry."

"That's OK, Beau."

Lincoln sat back in his seat and the pair began to rearrange their rumpled clothing. Notwithstanding Lincoln's kind words, Abraham could tell that his boyfriend was disappointed. Abraham placed his hand lovingly on the side of Lincoln's face.

"Soon, I promise."

"Whenever you're ready."

They made their goodbyes and Abraham quickly went inside. As soon as he shut the bedroom door behind him, Abraham whipped off his jeans, laid down on his bed and, after a very brief bout of expert handiwork, promptly came all over himself at the thought of Lincoln...and a little of Officer Ford if he was to be honest.

Lincoln doesn't need to know.

* * *

Abraham hadn't made any great announcements about his sexuality at school but anyone who didn't know by now would've had to be blind or completely in denial, seeing how he and Lincoln always walked hand in hand through the school with an almost sickening, loved-up aura about them. They were certainly one of the school's hottest new topics of discussion, with the gossip mills buzzing with news of their coupledom.

Dating Lincoln had also had a positive effect on Abraham's personality, as it had made him far more outgoing and confident in himself. As clichéd as it sounded, even to Abraham himself, it felt as if he'd left the shadows and was finally taking his place on the center stage.

Abraham hadn't been the only one to notice the change, as he found out one afternoon when he was showering after swim training. He was alone in the group showers with the steam billowing around him, smiling to himself and singing one of his favorite Adrian Lux songs. His voice echoed in the large tiled area, as he lathered himself up.

"We don't sleep when the sun goes down. We don't waste no precious time, all my friends in the loop. Making up for teenage crime..."

"Not bad, maybe you should try out for the Glee club," came a familiar voice from right behind Abraham.

Startled, Abraham jumped and spun around quickly, losing his balance. He was certain that he was going to go crashing to the floor when a pair of strong hands caught him.

"Whoa, careful there, Abe."

His heart beating wildly from the near miss, Abraham looked up to see that the newcomer, and subsequent savior, was the quarterback, Jonas.

"Thanks," mumbled Abraham, embarrassed over his clumsiness.

"No problem, you should be more careful though," replied Jonas with a cocky grin.

Jonas released his grip on Abraham's arm and stepped back to turn on the shower right next to Abraham.

Why did he take the one that's so close?

"Yeah...I know. You just startled me that's all," stated Abraham, ashamed of his skittishness.

"Sorry, I didn't mean to."

"That's OK. I probably shouldn't have been singing so loud."

"Nah, I liked it."

As Jonas began to lather himself up, Abraham looked away and started to rinse himself off. He was a little puzzled to say the least. This was probably the longest conversation that he'd had with the quarterback in all the years he'd known him. Indeed,

Abraham had actually had far more interaction with Jonas' younger sister, Julie, who was co-captain of the girls' swim team. Today, there was just something in the way that Jonas was looking at him that seemed...different. When Abraham's budding sexuality had begun to bloom inside him a few years ago, he'd had a ridiculously huge crush on Jonas, understandably drawn in by the quarterback's chiseled good looks – as had a great many others. Of course, he hadn't thought about Jonas in that way since he'd met Lincoln.

"So, how are you and Lincoln going?" asked Jonas in an off-hand manner.

"Good."

"Yeah, you look good together."

Is it me or is he being really weird?

"Thanks."

Abraham was glad that others thought that he and Lincoln were well suited, not that he needed confirmation but it was still comforting nevertheless. Even so, Abraham was confused by Jonas' sudden interest in his relationship.

"You know you seem different these days."

"Do I?" asked Abraham, his curiosity aroused.

"Yeah, more sure of yourself...it's kinda hot," remarked Jonas, his eyes not leaving Abraham's body.

"Thanks...I guess."

Where the hell is this going?

"How's Penny?"

"Oh, we're off again. Drama, drama, drama... sometimes I think I'd be better off sticking just to boys," chuckled Jonas.

"Oh?"

"Yeah, maybe I should try to find someone more like you."

Jonas had been slowly edging closer to Abraham during their conversation, so that he was now barely a few inches away. As much as Abraham tried not to he couldn't help but notice Jonas' slick, muscular body and his plump manhood that seemed to be very much in the process of waking up. His own member had also swelled up in response to being so close to his former crush. A few months ago this very situation would have been Abraham's total fantasy and while he was unquestionably still attracted to Jonas, it wasn't what he now desired on an emotional level.

"I...don't...I...umm..." Abraham was nervous, confused and very much lost for words, and couldn't look Jonas in the eye.

Jonas reached over and put his hand on Abraham's cheek to lift his gaze back towards him. Abraham could see the blatant desire in his eyes.

"Why are you so nervous?" murmured Jonas.

"I'm not...I just..."

Jonas cut off Abraham by moving forward to give him a very hungry kiss. Their wet naked bodies pressed together. It felt wonderful to Abraham, for a second, but then he remembered who he was kissing and he forcefully pushed Jonas away.

"I have a boyfriend!"

"So? I wasn't going to tell him...besides, it's not like you didn't enjoy it," remarked Jonas as he gestured to Abraham's prominent erection.

"That's not the point. You shouldn't have kissed me!"

"Don't be such a prude."

Jonas stepped in towards Abraham again and drew him in close once more. The sensation of the quarterback's powerful grip excited Abraham far more than he liked and made him hesitate slightly, before he recovered his senses and made to get away. Thanks to the slipperiness of his body, combined with a sudden burst of strength, Abraham managed to push Jonas off of him. Before Jonas reestablished his hold, Abraham made his escape and rushed out of the showers to his locker.

"Hey, come back. I was just having fun!"

Abraham didn't reply as he rapidly toweled off and changed, all the while his thoughts were filled with anger, shock and guilt. He was just rushing out of the change room as Jonas reentered toweling himself off.

"Why you running off, Abe?"

Abraham merely shot Jonas a dark look in response and beat a hasty exit.

How could I cheat on Lincoln? Why am I such an idiot! Did I somehow encourage Jonas? What have I done?

* * *

The next day, Abraham repeatedly berated himself while he waited at home for Lincoln to show up. He'd spent a restless night wracked with guilt and decided that he needed to confess everything and just accept whatever punishment he was due – even if that meant losing his boyfriend. Abraham was so ashamed of his actions he hadn't even told Topher of his wrongdoing.

What have I done? He's the best thing that ever happened to me. I should have known it wouldn't last. I'm such a loser!

Thankfully, his family was going to be gone all day at the annual Port Davinica Horse Fair – a passion of his sister's – so he had the house to himself to perform the unpleasant deed. He'd called Lincoln earlier and invited him over but hadn't mentioned anything about needing to talk.

I can't do it over the phone.

Before too long, Abraham heard the familiar sound of Lincoln's jeep pulling into the driveway. He took a deep breath to help calm his nerves and opened the door to see Lincoln looking as handsome as ever. Before saying a word, Abraham went and greeted his boyfriend with a warm, loving kiss.

I may not get another chance.

"Hey, Beau. Now that's a fine welcome." Lincoln then furrowed his brow, apparently noticing that something was wrong with his boyfriend. "Y'OK?"

"No…no, I'm not," replied Abraham miserably.

"Why, what's wrong? Have I done something?" demanded Lincoln, panic showing in his eyes.

"No! Of course not…let's just go inside."

Lincoln obediently followed Abraham inside and soon the lads were installed on the sofa in the living room, sitting uncomfortably together. After a minute, Lincoln broke the awkward silence.

"Are ya going to tell me what's going on?"

"I'm…I'm an asshole and I don't deserve you," bleated Abraham before breaking down in tears.

"Hey now, Beau. Whatever it is, it can't be all that bad." Lincoln instinctually moved forward to comfort Abraham, putting his arm around his boyfriend's shoulders.

"You're going to hate me!"

"Why don't ya tell me and I can be the judge of that."

Abraham pulled away from Lincoln and began to tearfully explain what had happened with Jonas the day before, while his boyfriend listened attentively. When he'd finished, Abraham looked up at his boyfriend expecting to see betrayal and anger in his eyes but was surprised to see neither. Instead, Lincoln was grinning and looking at him curiously.

"Is that all?" asked Lincoln, a rather bemused expression crossing his face.

"Yeah...but it's bad enough. I've ruined everything!"

"No, ya haven't. It's fine."

Abraham was incredulous. It was not at all how he expected Lincoln to react.

"But...how can you forgive me? I cheated on you!"

"Ya didn't do anything wrong. Look, I believe you when you say that you didn't start it. Jonas did the same thing to me, don't you remember?"

Abraham had actually completely forgotten about walking in on Lincoln and Jonas in the exact same compromising position only a few months beforehand.

"Come here," said Lincoln drawing Abraham into a strong embrace. "You'll have to do a lot more than that to get rid of me, Mister."

A wonderful sensation of calm contentment replaced Abraham's feelings of guilt and shame. He reveled in the sensation of Lincoln's muscular arms wrapped around him and soaked up the warmth of his boyfriend's embrace.

"Would ya feel better if I went and beat up Jonas for trying to steal my man?" joked Lincoln, in a show of mock bravado.

"Yes! Although staying right here and holding me works too," murmured Abraham as he snuggled in closer to Lincoln's chest.

"Works for me, Beau."

After half an hour of cuddling and quiet conversation, the loved-up lads retreated to the backyard and proceeded to splash about together in the heated swimming pool. Even though it was the depths of winter, the day was bright and clear with the sun streaming down into the backyard, although it offered little in the way of warmth. Around them the ground was covered in a blanket of fine white powdery snow, as the steam steadily rose off the water. Lincoln was wearing a pair of navy-blue swimmers that he'd borrowed from Abraham, although they were almost a bit too snug. The material was stretched tight due to Lincoln's more generously proportioned posterior and it was uncertain how long they'd continue to contain his ample attributes.

They splashed and grabbed at one another, their carefree laughter ringing through the backyard, with Abraham's confession all but forgotten. In a sudden show of strength, Lincoln pinned Abraham up against the side of the pool and their faces came together into a passionate kiss. Their slippery bodies ground up against one another, which in turn caused both their cocks to swell to their full hardness. The kissing and groping became even more ardent as they half floated towards the shallow end where the stairs led into the pool. Lincoln lifted

Abraham up onto the top step so that he was half out of the water. He yanked down Abraham's swimmers exposing the hard erection contained within. Grasping the manhood in his hand, Lincoln slowly jacked it as his other hand cupped and gently massaged Abraham's low hanging balls.

"We shouldn't...someone might see," protested Abraham, but made no moves to stop his boyfriend's actions. "God, it feels so good."

"Well, wait till ya feel this, Beau."

And with that Lincoln moved forward and put his mouth to the tip of Abraham's cockhead and swirled his tongue around, lapping up the slightly salty precum that was leaking from the eye.

"Fuck!" exclaimed Abraham.

It was the first time a mouth had come anywhere near his cock and he thought he may explode straight away but somehow managed to hold himself back.

Why did I wait so damn long!

Lincoln then displayed his well-practiced skill by moving his head forward to swallow the manhood whole, taking all of Abraham's nine inches down deep into his throat – his gag reflex seemingly non-existent. Any thoughts of being caught by nosy neighbors had vanished from Abraham's mind with his focus purely on the incredible sensation of warmth and pleasure surrounding his manhood. He grasped at the back of Lincoln's head and shoulders while moaning his appreciation.

Lincoln slowly came back up, his tongue leisurely circling the shaft, causing Abraham to squirm and gasp in satisfaction. When he reached the tip, Lincoln nibbled softly on Abraham's thick foreskin, sending little electric shocks of pleasure all over Abraham's tensed body.

It was more than he could take and Abraham suddenly shuddered as his orgasm began to burst forth.

"Linc...I'm cumming..."

Instead of backing off, as Abraham thought he would, Lincoln took the shaft into his mouth once more and greedily slurped down the delicious cream. Abraham's body was wracked with shudders of ecstasy as each powerful spurt of cum was released. He'd never had such a sensation of pleasure in his life. His cockhead became extremely sensitive and Abraham tried to gently push his boyfriend's mouth away but Lincoln refused to budge, apparently determined to keep licking and sucking until he had extracted every last salty-sweet drop.

When Lincoln had drained him dry, he moved up and planted a sweet kiss on Abraham's waiting mouth.

"That was..." whispered Abraham.

"Yeah it was," agreed Lincoln, a satisfied grin covering his mouth.

Lincoln smiled and kissed Abraham again. Abraham could taste the faint remnants of his own seed, although it wasn't the first time, as he'd already satisfied his curiosity a few years beforehand on that matter. Feeling adventurous, Abraham decided to take things further.

"Can I have yours?" inquired Abraham, although he was already sure of the answer.

"It's all yours, Beau."

Wasting no time, Abraham maneuvered Lincoln into a standing position, with his legs still mostly in the water, and ripped down the swimwear. Lincoln's erection sprang free and came tantalizingly close to Abraham's face. It was the same length as Abraham's, but slighter thicker with a large vein running along the left side. He admired the beauty of it, especially how darkly colored it appeared – almost black – in comparison to the rest of Lincoln's body.

A generous amount of precum was oozing from the engorged glans and Abraham's mouth watered in anticipation. He imagined that he wouldn't be anywhere near as good as Lincoln had been but he meant to give it his best shot. Abraham approached it tentatively, and grasped the erection in his right hand and then pulled it towards his open mouth, while Lincoln's strong hands gently caressed the back of his head. He gave the cockhead an exploratory lick, the precum sliding across his tongue and exciting his taste buds.

Mmm…so sweet.

Abraham then ran his tongue along the underside of the fleshy shaft, down to the large, pendulous chocolate-colored balls. He savored the texture of the skin, as he brought his tongue back along the length of the erect manhood to the tip. Taking care to keep his teeth well clear, Abraham opened his mouth wide and swallowed the swollen cockhead, letting it rest in his mouth, as more of the delicious precum leaked onto his tongue and down his throat. Ever so slowly, Abraham began to bob up and down on the shaft, taking it a little deeper with each downward movement of his head. He gagged a little at first but soon adjusted to the feeling of the substantial amount of meat in his mouth. At present he could only get halfway down the shaft but he certainly had ambitions of deep-throating the full length of it.

Maybe not today, but soon.

His other hand played with Lincoln's heavy balls, enjoying their smooth feel in his hand as he gently massaged and tugged on them.

"Damn, Beau. Ya sure this is your first time," gasped Lincoln.

Abraham nodded, his mouth still exceedingly full of his boyfriend's manhood.

"Well you're certainly a mighty quick learner."

The words of praise pleased Abraham greatly and he went about his task with even more vigor. He came off the shaft and licked all around the base of the cock, coating the whole area in a thin film of saliva before taking the balls into his mouth one at a time. Above him Lincoln, wriggled and moaned his enjoyment. Abraham went back to sucking on the shaft while jacking it with slow, deliberate movements. It didn't take too long before his hard work paid off and he felt Lincoln's body tense up ahead of an orgasm.

"I'm close," grunted Lincoln, his legs beginning to shake.

Abraham moved forward taking the shaft far into his mouth, as he wanted to do as his boyfriend had and drink down the load. He wasn't prepared, however, for the mammoth amount of cum that erupted from the throbbing manhood. Valiantly, Abraham swallowed as much as he could but some still escaped his mouth and dripped down his chin and into the water.

When he was fully spent, Lincoln dragged Abraham up, lovingly licked the excess cum away and kissed his boyfriend deeply. Abraham was overwhelmed with emotion and couldn't keep his feelings contained any more.

"I love you, Linc," gushed Abraham.

"I love you too, Abe."

It was the first time either of the pair had said the words out loud. Becoming aware of the cold once more, the duo sank back down into the pool, holding one another as they lay on the stairs, the heated water caressing their spent bodies.

"Y'OK, Beau?" asked Lincoln, tenderly.

"Better than ever." Abraham had a wide grin plastered on his face. "I wouldn't mind doing *more*…later though."

"Sounds fine to me. Like I said, I'm happy to go as slow as ya like and I'm not going anywhere."

"Good, 'cause I'm never letting you go."

"That suits me fine, kind Sir."

Abraham held Lincoln tight against his body. Naturally, this then progressed into a renewed bout of fiery kisses and their members soon rehardened ready for action. It looked like there was going to be a repeat performance when they were unexpectedly disturbed by the slamming of car doors, followed shortly after by Megan's voice, yelling at her parents.

"I HATE BOTH OF YOU!"

This was followed directly by the stern voice of Abraham's father booming through the house and out to the terrace.

"Megan Elizabeth Chadwick, you get your butt to your room and stay there until you can behave like a proper young lady and not a spoiled brat."

Another door slammed shut and the boys, not wanting to be caught, desperately scrambled to pull up their swimmers, which were still resting around their ankles. Fortunately, Abraham's parents seemed to be preoccupied with their delinquent daughter and didn't come outside. The boys hopped back out of the pool and wrapped themselves up in extra-large, fluffy towels to keep them warm – and protect their modesty seeing their erections were persistently in full force.

Walking in the backdoor, the lads encountered Abraham's mother making herself a coffee in the kitchen.

"Oh, hi, Lincoln. Sorry you had to hear that," said Sheila, clearly embarrassed by her daughter's behavior.

"It's fine, Ma'am. One of my little cousins back home is way worse." Lincoln laughed and put her at ease.

"Her poor parents. Are you staying for dinner, Lincoln?"

"I'd love to Ma'am."

"Now, Lincoln. I've told you before, call me Sheila, please. I hope you boys enjoyed your swim".

"Yeah, we did, thanks very much," said Abraham, who could barely keep a straight face.

"Very much so," agreed Lincoln, with an impish smile.

The boys retreated upstairs to the warmth of the shower – separately unfortunately, as Abraham's parents weren't that enlightened. Contrary to their natural instincts, they managed to fight the overwhelming urge to continue their pool shenanigans and spent the rest of the afternoon on Abraham's bed watching reruns of Doctor Who. It would be fair to say, however, that Abraham's mind was far from focused on the adventures of the Time Lord and his plucky companion.

I can't wait for the next time!

* * *

Exactly one week later, Abraham was locked in his bathroom, fussing about in front of the mirror, with his stomach full of bears – well, they felt far too big to be butterflies. He was getting ready for his Valentine's Day dinner with Lincoln, which was going to be special for more than just the momentous occasion of the first time Abraham actually had a partner. Following their exploits in Abraham's backyard, the boys had talked a lot and together they'd decided that tonight would be the night.

I can do this. I love him, he loves me and it will be amazing!

He'd told Topher a few days beforehand and his best friend had been extremely supportive of his decision, if somewhat facetious.

"Bout time!" remarked Topher. "Pity I wasn't home when you guys were going at it in the pool. It would've been hot to watch."

"Perve!"

"You love it!"

"Maybe…I just hope that everything goes well. I mean the things we did in the pool were pretty awesome but I'm worried it might hurt when we do the other stuff."

Topher could easily see how anxious Abraham was and did his very best to reassure his best friend.

"Honestly, sex can be uncomfortable but it can also be the most fantastic experience. If you have a good and patient partner it'll all be fine. Trust me, I know. Eli was so good with me and I'm sure Lincoln will be for you too."

"I hope so."

Abraham pushed his apprehension aside and finished getting ready. He had on his only suit, a light-gray one he'd last worn to his aunt's wedding the year before. He had paired it with a cobalt-blue shirt and shiny black shoes.

I don't look too shabby.

With one final check in the mirror, Abraham was on his merry way. They had chosen Lincoln's house for the grand event, as his mom had gone away for the weekend with her sister, so they would have the place all to themselves. Topher had given Abraham a lift on his way out to his own Valentine's celebration with Eli.

"Don't do anything I wouldn't do," quipped Topher through the car window as he drove off.

Abraham walked up the front path and then hesitated nervously a moment before ringing the doorbell. Even though Abraham had been there quite a few times before, he knew this time was different. The door opened to reveal a smiling Lincoln who was also dressed in a suit – navy-blue with a crisp white shirt.

"Here," said Abraham, offering a large bouquet of red roses that he'd been concealing behind his back.

"Thanks, Beau." He accepted the flowers and then showed Abraham an identical bunch. "Great minds."

Lincoln placed the flowers on the side table and then took Abraham's hand to draw him inside. Once he'd shut the door behind them, Lincoln swept up Abraham into his solid arms for a long, loving kiss. When they finally broke apart, Lincoln ushered his boyfriend into the dining room where the table was aglow with candles and a bottle of champagne sat chilling in an ice bucket.

Abraham began to tear up slightly as he saw the effort Lincoln had gone to make their night special.

"It all looks amazing, Linc."

"Nothing's too good for ya, Beau."

Lincoln moved to the table and proceeded to uncork the champagne, which opened with a satisfying 'pop'. He took the two crystal flutes off the table and filled them before handing one to Abraham.

"May this be the first of many Valentines to come. To us!" toasted Lincoln.

"To us!" repeated Abraham, his face lit with happiness.

The lovebirds then sat down to enjoy the meal that Lincoln had lovingly prepared. He'd even included a few aphrodisiacs - smoked oysters, avocado topped with pine nuts drizzled in honey and chocolate-covered strawberries – not that the pair needed any help in that department.

He can cook for me forever!

The bears in Abraham's stomach had settled down somewhat – practically back to mere butterflies – but he was still full of nervous energy. The conversation remained light and gay as they ate, neither lad wanting to mention the impending event to come. When they'd finished eating Lincoln took Abraham by the hand and led him upstairs to his bedroom. From the door there was a trail of rose petals leading to the bed, which brought another swell of emotion to Abraham's heart.

"Linc, it's perfect!"

"Thanks, Beau."

Abraham noticed that Lincoln seemed to be almost as nervous as he was feeling himself – something that Abraham found sweet and wonderfully endearing. He couldn't believe that they were finally taking this huge step as a couple and hoped that it would only help to cement their love for one another.

At least he's done this before.

Together, they made their way to the bed and lay down on top of the duvet. Ever so tenderly, the boys came together and slowly peeled off each other's clothing, kissing all the while. The floor was soon littered with their suits and shirts, with only their underwear remaining on their writhing bodies. The few glasses of champagne had gone straight to Abraham's head making him slightly tipsy but he adored every fuzzy second of their encounter.

After a few minutes, Abraham started to feel nauseous. At first he put it down to nerves and too much champagne but the uncomfortable sensation increased and he suddenly sat bolt upright with alarm. It was then his stomach started to cramp severely and he realized that something was very wrong indeed.

"I'm going to be sick," he exclaimed, before rushing from the bed and into Lincoln's en suite.

"Abe?" called a worried Lincoln from the bed.

Fortunately, Abraham made it to the bathroom just in time, fell hard to his knees and then proceeded to projectile vomit into the toilet. He clutched at the ceramic bowl for support, as his body shuddered uncontrollably.

"Abe, what's going on? Are ya, OK?"

Lincoln had just joined him in the bathroom, his face brimming with concern.

"No, I feel..."

He didn't have time to finish his sentence before his stomach desperately tried to empty itself again.

"Hold on, I'll just get ya..." Lincoln stopped mid sentence his face grimaced in pain. "Oh, no, I..."

And with that he ran from the room to the bathroom down the hall. Moments later, Abraham could hear his boyfriend also violently voiding the contents of his stomach. It wasn't the bonding experience he'd had in mind for their night, although he didn't have too much time to dwell on it as his own sickness took hold once again.

The next hour passed in a wretched haze of cramps, sweating and heaving. In between bouts of illness, Lincoln managed to call his neighbor, who was fortunately a doctor, to come and rescue them from their misery. She arrived five minutes later with a small, black leather bag stocked with emergency medical supplies. Even in his sorry state, Abraham was a little taken aback by how beautiful the good doctor was, with her arresting clear gray eyes, waist-length midnight black hair, porcelain-white skin and a lithe figure. Not that he was considering switching teams but he could still appreciate the attractiveness of the fairer sex on occasion.

I didn't know that doctors could look that good outside of TV soaps!

"Oh, you poor boys," remarked Dr. Madeline Hastings upon seeing the state of them. "Looks like food poisoning to me. Have you eaten anything unusual?"

"Only the smoked oysters," admitted Lincoln.

"That'll do it."

"I'm so sorry, Abe. I thought I cooked the oysters properly but I musta messed up," apologized Lincoln, shame written all over his sickly face.

"It's OK, but please stop talking about the food."

Dr. Hastings soon injected the lads with strong anti-nausea medication and stayed with them until their convulsions had stopped a short time later.

"Keep up your fluids and call me if you need me. I'll swing by in the morning before work to see how you're both faring."

"Thanks, Dr. Hastings," said Lincoln gratefully.

"Yes, thanks so much," added an extremely pale-looking Abraham.

"I'll see you out," offered Lincoln, ever the gentleman even in the midst of his malady.

"Don't be silly. Rest here, I can see myself out."

After she'd left them alone, Abraham and Lincoln helped each other into the shower and let the warm water soothe their weary bodies. A good while later, they climbed wearily out and toweled each other off before heading back to the bedroom. The lads then spent the night in bed together, although there wasn't anything vaguely sexual about it. Cuddled up together and feeling like death, they soon drifted off into a fitful slumber.

The next morning, they lay together, feeling drained but at least well on the way to being better.

"I'm so sorry, Beau," apologized Lincoln mournfully, for the umpteenth time.

"You really have to stop saying that."

"But I ruined our night; I wanted it to be perfect for ya."

"Well, it was certainly memorable," teased Abraham with a small laugh that he instantly regretted as his stomach was still sore from all the cramping. "Besides, we have time to try again."

"Ya still want to, after all I just put ya through?"

"Of course I do, doofus. I love you and can't wait to give myself to you fully."

"Glad to hear it."

They snuggled into one another and then spent the rest of the day dozing off and on – food the very last thing on their mind.

* * *

It took a few days for the boys to feel back to their usual healthy selves but they were thankfully soon able to joke about their disastrous date. That being said, both were very keen to try again. Sadly, finding an opportunity to have a house all to themselves that also worked in with both Abraham's busy swimming schedule and Lincoln's cheerleading and glee club commitments, was proving rather difficult. They still spent as much time as possible, attending each other's after school activities when they could. Abraham particularly liked watching his boyfriend go through the routines during his cheerleading practice, as Lincoln's habitual pair of sky-blue tights highlighted every last inch of his well-built lower half. The effect on Abraham was quite predictable and he often found himself having to adjust his growing crotch several times during the proceedings.

In the meantime, another important matter had taken precedence – starting to plan for their futures. By the end of March, the first round of acceptance letters had already been sent out and the news was mixed. Abraham and Lincoln had applied to schools before they'd started dating so their relationship hadn't been a consideration for either of them at the time. It also didn't help that their career paths were wildly different. Abraham harbored a strong desire to become a marine biologist, his love of water permeating every area of his life, whereas Lincoln dreamt of treading the stage and had been looking at various university theater programs. The only school that they'd jointly applied to was the locally situated Port Davinica University, to which Abraham had already been accepted. Lincoln, however, was still on a lengthy waiting list. Before he'd met Lincoln, the idea of going away to college had been exciting to Abraham, but it seemed that the undesirable option of a long distance relationship might be their only solution.

"I want to stay with you," commented Abraham sadly, after they'd compared acceptance letters.

"Well hopefully I'll get off the waiting list and we can both go to PDU," reassured Lincoln.

"Yeah, but what if that doesn't happen."

"No need to worry that handsome head of yours about it just yet. We have time, Beau."

Despite Lincoln's confidence, Abraham was vexed. The thought of being separated so soon into their relationship gnawed at Abraham but he knew there was nothing he could do. He didn't want to stand in the way of Lincoln's dreams, even if that meant he had to leave to attend school away from the city.

Will our relationship survive a separation?

It was only by chance that he'd even applied to Port Davinica University in the first place. His preferred school had been the prestigious Oxer University in San Francisco, whose marine biology program was considered one of the best in the country. His 4.0 grade point average and athletic achievements pretty much guaranteed him a spot, so he'd only considered applying to PDU to appease his parents' desire that he have at least one 'safety school'.

To begin with, Abraham hadn't really thought it to be a serious option. His opinion had changed somewhat after he'd attended a career day the previous semester, when he'd had the pleasure of meeting Professor Marco Gatti. He wasn't at all what Abraham had expected a professor to look like. In his early thirties, with tousled black hair, brown eyes, tanned Italian skin and a tall, lean build; he looked more like a model than an educator.

They'd chatted at length about the professor's recent work studying the declining walrus populations in Iceland. To be honest, Abraham had been a tad smitten with the professor and had fawned more than a little.

"That's so interesting, Professor," gushed Abraham.

"Please, I prefer Marco. You should definitely think about the course at PDU. It would be great to have more curious, engaged minds like yours in my class," enthused Marco with a warm smile.

Abraham had melted a little at the attention and blushed noticeably, not that the Professor remarked upon it. His little crush had caused Abraham to further investigate the course offered by the University and he discovered that it was comparable to his top choice. He'd dutifully sent off his application, without giving it too much more thought, which in hindsight may have turned out to be quite fortuitous, given the current circumstances.

What'll we do if he doesn't get in?

* * *

The relationship between Abraham and Lincoln continued to grow stronger over the coming weeks, even if they had yet to consummate it properly. Abraham was thankful for his boyfriend's patience but he didn't want to keep him waiting indefinitely and time appeared to be racing by at an alarming rate. Indeed, before they knew it was Spring Break, which, as it turned out, provided the lads with a much-needed opportunity.

Abraham and Lincoln had been invited by Tobias to spend the break camping with some of their fellow students in Christie National Park, a few hours drive east from Port Davinica. In the end, there were an even dozen in the group, including Jonas and Penny, who seemed to be very much back on again...for now. The rest of their party was made up of the usual suspects – Lydia, Topher, Eli, Annika, Kathryn, Austin and Cassidy. With much organization, four cars were loaded with people and supplies and they set off early Friday morning on the relatively short road trip to the mountains. After checking in at the park station with Ranger Masaki Ito – a strapping, outdoorsy man of Japanese heritage – the group made their way to a fairly secluded spot by a medium-sized, crystal-blue lake that overlooked a lush valley. The sweet smell of wildflowers hung in the air and all around them the glory of spring was in full force – singing birds, buzzing bees and other amorous woodland creatures at play.

The one downside to being so isolated was the lack of amenities. Fortunately, Tobias had had the forethought to bring a shovel for their toiletry needs and a portable shower, which he capably secured to a nearby grouping of trees – his woodland skills undoubtedly due to his family's habit of camping every summer. Unfortunately, it did mean bracingly cold showers unless they wanted to go to the trouble of heating the water each time, which none of the group were particularly bothered with seeing the weather was so warm. While the mornings and evenings still had a slight nip to them, the days themselves were pleasant enough.

The freedom of being away from the supervision of parents leant the trip a festive, party air. In fact, their situation had all the markings of a horror film in the making – carefree teens in the woods just ripe for the picking. Mercifully, that was the stuff of fiction…or so Abraham told himself whenever he heard an unexpected rustling outside the tent in the middle of the night.

Throughout the week the friends indulged in a good deal of physical activity – hiking about the surrounding mountains, as well as swimming in the lake and the endurance training of drinking around the campfire of a nighttime. Predictably, said drinking led to a loosening of inhibitions, not that this particular group of teenagers had been repressed in the first place. There was all manner of alcohol-inspired behavior, such as skinny-dipping and a nightly game of musical sleeping bags…evidenced by the various moans and groans heard throughout the night and the sight of shame-faced people sneakily trying to return to their own tents of a morning.

Despite Topher's kind offer of shared accommodation, and to ensure that he and Lincoln had a modicum of privacy, Abraham had borrowed a generously proportioned two-man tent from his parents. He was keen to spend as much time with Lincoln as possible, exploring and enjoying each other's bodies. Since their first play in the pool there had been quite a bit more fellatio, nipple play and groping, mostly in Lincoln's jeep, but that had been the extent of it. Abraham had been frightened about doing much more in such an exposed setting after their embarrassing encounter with Officer Ford. Here in the woods, however, there was little chance of being interrupted, except by their friends. Even though Abraham was enjoying himself with the group, he still thought it would have been ideal if it were just the two of them alone for the week.

We'd just spend the entire time fucking! Damn, that'd be good. Maybe, next time.

The boys had become increasingly daring in their nighttime rituals, over the course of the week, progressing from passionate kissing and mutual masturbation into hungry sixty-nines, gentle fingering and a touch of rimming. By the end of the week, Abraham decided that he couldn't bear to wait any longer to become a man – luckily they'd brought along the necessary supplies, just in case. Not that making love in a tent would be as romantic as he'd hoped his first time would be, but his carnal needs were far outweighing his starry-eyed ones. Truly, by this point his cock didn't care if he lost his virginity in a dingy back alley full of horny sailors but his heart remained a little more discerning. When he told Lincoln of his decision, his boyfriend had been excited but cautious.

"I just want to make sure that it's special for ya, Beau."

"As long as I'm with you, it'll be perfect...minus the food poisoning of course," quipped Abraham.

"No more oysters, I swear!"

That night, the boys retired earlier than the rest of their raucous group and were soon sheltered away in their tent quietly kissing one another and gradually undressing. Before too long, they were completely naked, their erections poking into one another as they writhed together and rolled around the tent trying to contain their sounds of satisfaction – they didn't want to attract the attention of their friends, after all. Hands, mouths and tongues went seeking for pleasure and soon the boys were locked into a fervent sixty-nine. Abraham adored having his face pushed into his boyfriend's crotch while the wide manhood was wedged inside his throat, coupled with the glorious sensation of Lincoln pleasuring him at the same time. He gripped Lincoln's buttocks, his nails lightly digging into the plump orbs as Abraham pulled his boyfriend in even closer. His practice over the past months had paid off and Abraham was now able to deep-throat Lincoln's substantial inches with his gag reflex barely triggering at all – quite the feat, indeed.

All of a sudden, Lincoln broke free of their passionate coupling and flipped Abraham on his back. He spread Abraham's legs wide apart and shoved his face inside the exposed hole, rimming it with an urgent longing. Abraham loved the sensation of the tongue swirling around and inside his sensitive hole, causing him to gasp in delight at the expert technique. His hands grasped forcefully at the back of Lincoln's head, his fingers running through the soft, tightly-wound black curls.

After a while, Abraham pulled Lincoln upwards into a ferocious kiss. Their naked bodies grappled together, as the temperature inside the tent continued to climb, filling the air with the intoxicating musk of men at play.

"My turn!" announced Abraham, as he flipped Lincoln face down on the sleeping bag.

Abraham jumped on top of him and then licked and kissed his way down Lincoln's broad, muscular back, until he reached the invitingly round bubble butt. He lightly bit the cheeks, and teased them by running his tongue along the edges of the crease between them. Abraham was tentative to go further, as while he'd already digitally penetrated Lincoln several times, Abraham had never rimmed him. Truthfully, even though he knew how amazing it felt to receive it, he was slightly hesitant about the possibility of unpleasant surprises. Throwing caution to the wind – and safe in the knowledge that they'd both had showers earlier that evening – Abraham took the plunge. Abraham moved his face down and spread the fleshy cheeks wide and licked around the edges of the entrance. He blew on the sensitive hole causing Lincoln to squirm. Gaining in confidence, Abraham licked over the hole and then took little stabs inside, gradually widening the hole to get his tongue in even deeper. The taste was musky, but not unpleasant, and Abraham's hunger grew. He shoved his face deep into the crevice, extending his swirling tongue further into the passage.

Fuck, I love this!

Abraham alternated between using his fingers and tongue to pleasure Lincoln, starting with one, then two and finally a third digit. His boyfriend grunted his appreciation and Abraham adored the way the sphincter kept clamping down and squeezing his fingers, already imagining how incredible it would feel around his member.

Lincoln turned to look back over his shoulder at Abraham.

"I want ya in me, Beau," demanded Lincoln, his eyes burning with need.

"Your wish is my command."

Abraham couldn't believe it was finally going to happen. He grabbed the lubricant from his toiletry bag and lubed himself up, before coating Lincoln's welcoming entrance thoroughly.

"Take it slow, it's been a while," murmured Lincoln, as he tilted his hips up to receive his boyfriend.

"Don't worry, I'm going to make this last as long as possible."

"I love ya, Beau."

"Me, too!"

Abraham's glans grazed across Lincoln's perineum as he lined up his bare cockhead with the slick entrance. They'd both been tested at the local clinic and had decided that they trusted one another enough to forgo condoms. As he began to slowly push, Abraham could feel the warmth coming from the passage. He was just beginning to breach the ring when he was disturbed by a sudden voice from outside the entrance to the tent.

"Abe. I really need to talk to you!"

It was Topher in a very obvious state of distress.

Dammit to hell!

"Umm…it's really not a good time. Can you come back in a bit?" asked Abraham hopefully.

"Please, Abe," pleaded Topher.

"Wait a sec."

So close!

Lincoln turned over on his back to face Abraham with a pained expression that matched Abraham's own growing sense of annoyance and frustration. Stretching up, Lincoln gave Abraham a gentle kiss.

"Why don't the gods want us to have sex?" lamented Abraham quietly.

"It's OK," whispered Lincoln, a hint of disappointment in his eyes.

"Stay there, Mister. I promise I won't be long."

"I won't move a muscle."

Abraham shoved on a t-shirt and shorts, doing his best to hide his raging erection. When he saw Topher's red and puffy eyes, however, Abraham correctly guessed it wouldn't be settled quickly.

"What's wrong?" asked Abraham, far more patiently than he was feeling.

"Eli and I had a fight, he…" Topher stopped when he noticed the obvious bulge in Abraham's shorts and apparently realized what he'd interrupted. "Oh no, I'm so sorry, Abe."

"Nah, it's OK," replied Abraham, unconvincingly.

"But I interrupted you in the middle of…" he said raising his eyebrows pointedly.

"Well…yeah, but I'm sure we'll have another opportunity. Now tell me what happened."

"OK, only if you're sure?" Abraham gestured for Topher to continue. "Eli had been gone for a while so I went looking for him and I found him rolling around half-naked with Jonas and Penny in their tent! They were just kissing but it sure looked like they were going to go a hell of a lot further."

Always Jonas!

"I thought you and Eli were pretty open about that stuff," questioned Abraham, a little confused as to how this differed from their normal behavior.

"Honestly, all that stuff about playing around is just talk. Sure, I don't mind him kissing other people sometimes, that's fun and I like doing it too, but we have an agreement that anything more is kept only for each other!"

While Abraham couldn't fathom the idea of being comfortable with Lincoln kissing anyone else he didn't feel like he was in a position to judge his friend.

To each their own.

"Can I sleep in with you guys tonight? I just can't be around Eli right now."

"Hold on a sec."

Abraham poked his head in the tent and gave Lincoln an apologetic look. Lincoln just smiled back with an understanding regard and nodded his answer to the unspoken question. Abraham was beginning to think that he might be cursed but realized that friendship was probably more important than fornication.

For tonight at least.

After waiting until Lincoln had clothed himself, Abraham let Topher into the tent. Abraham gave his best friend his sleeping bag, choosing to share Lincoln's himself. It wasn't how he wanted the night to end, but drifting off to sleep while being held in Lincoln's arms wasn't so bad. Besides he knew that they would consummate their love in the near future.

Very soon…

* * *

Two weeks later, Abraham was in the pool doing laps with his squad. They were practicing every day, twice a day, in preparation for the upcoming State championships. They had already aced the local competitions and the squad was well on track to take home the trophy for the third year in a row. Unfortunately, this hadn't left any time for Abraham and Lincoln to become intimate. On a positive note, the reason behind their last aborted attempt had been happily resolved the following day by a thoroughly repentant Eli and a forgiving Topher. Abraham was relieved and glad to see them reunited but took comfort in the fact that it would never be an issue in his own relationship.

I couldn't do that to Lincoln...or him me.

Abraham was wrecked; feeling dead tired and awfully pleased that practice was just about over. His body ached and he had the impression of being thoroughly waterlogged. He couldn't wait to shower off and be ferried home by his faithful boyfriend.

Early night tonight, again! I just wish I wasn't so exhausted.

A small crowd was watching the practice session from the stands, mostly members of the cheer squad and some teachers. Abraham had finished his last lap and was preparing to get out of the pool just behind Tobias. Looking up, Abraham appreciated the view of his co-captain's red and blue swimwear stretched across the pleasingly plump buttocks. Even though Abraham was wildly in love with Lincoln it didn't mean he'd suddenly become immune to the appeal of others – especially when he'd had his hands on them before, albeit briefly.

Abraham had just placed his right foot on the top step when Tobias suddenly slipped on the wet tiles, sending his arms flailing as he tried to right himself. Unfortunately for Abraham, Tobias' right elbow smacked him square in the face, which in turn caused him to lose grip on the railing of the stairs. As Abraham fell awkwardly backwards, his head caught the corner of the pool before he hit the water. A sharp, searing pain immediately engulfed the left side of his head and the world seemed to gradually fade away into blackness.

The next thing to penetrate Abraham's consciousness was the impression of faint voices calling out to him – or at least he thought they were. It was a most odd sensation, as they seemed to come from very far away, as if he was in a tunnel or under water. Try as he might, Abraham couldn't really discern what they were saying. He suddenly began to panic and tried to move but found that his body wasn't cooperating.

What's going on? Why can't I move? Am I dead?

The voices slowly began growing louder and louder, forming a babbling choir. Through the noise, Abraham realized that he could understand more of what was being said.

"Lie still, Abraham."

"Abe, can you hear me?"

"Oh my God! He's bleeding *so* much!"

"Somebody call 911!"

"Wake up, Beau. Come back to me."

Light began to seep through his eyelids as Abraham struggled to open them. At first, all he could see was a colorful blur hovering above him. His vision was extremely hazy and seemed to be fluttering. Little by little, it became clearer and Abraham could see that the blur was in fact a circle of worried faces, the most prominent of these being that of his boyfriend.

Lincoln's eyes were glistening with the start of tears and his complexion looked decidedly ashen. Abraham had an overwhelming desire to comfort his boyfriend and tried to sit up but immediately felt woozy and slumped backwards.

"Abraham, I need you to stay still. You've got a nasty gash to your head. We've staunched the bleeding but we need to wait for the paramedics to arrive." Coach Whiting commanded in his standard, authoritative voice.

"Please, Beau, don't move," added Lincoln.

Abraham's mind was still foggy and he was more than a little bewildered. He couldn't really remember anything more than swimming laps.

"Wh...wha...what happened?"

"I'm so sorry, Abe. Man, it's all my fault!" declared Tobias, his visage clouded with anguish and guilt.

"It was just an accident. Everything will be fine. No need for any one to blame themselves," reassured Coach Whiting, in an obvious effort to keep both his star swimmers calm.

Abraham was still befuddled, his throbbing head making it difficult for him to concentrate. The one thing he could understand was the heartening presence of Lincoln by his side, holding his hand in a comforting grip.

He's such a good boyfriend.

Before too long, the paramedics arrived and swiftly assessed the situation. They replaced the towel that had been pressed against his head with a clean bandage. Abraham was then asked a series of questions by the paramedics, which he did his best to answer in spite of the pain raging in his head. Seemingly satisfied with the answers, they eased Abraham into a seated position.

"Can you follow this light with your eyes?" asked the ruggedly handsome, blond paramedic.

Abraham did his best to comply but the pounding in his head was starting to make him feel nauseous. It didn't help that the paramedic's flowing blond hair and Nordic features made Abraham think of Thor.

I wonder if he has a big hammer?

"Good. Your pupils look fine but we need to get you to the hospital for stitches and some scans just to see that everything's A OK. Do you think you can stand?"

"I'll try."

He unsteadily got to his feet with a paramedic either side and a very anxious-looking Lincoln standing nearby. When he got up, Abraham turned his head and saw that the tiles where he had been laying were covered in dark, pinkish-colored water, due to his excessive bleeding. The sight immediately caused his stomach to lurch and the accompanying light-headedness saw him nearly faint dead away.

"Whoa, there. We've got you," said the other paramedic, a plain, capable-looking man with wire-rimmed glasses.

The paramedics kept him supported as they led him out to the ambulance, with a small group of concerned onlookers following their progress. They soon had him loaded up in the ambulance and were preparing to head to the nearest hospital – Sacred Heart General.

"We can only take one of you in the ambulance with us," instructed the blond paramedic.

"Lincoln, why don't you go with Abe and I'll drive anyone else who wants to go to the hospital in the school van."

"Thanks, Coach Whiting," gushed a clearly grateful Lincoln.

Half an hour later, Abraham was sitting in a small cubicle. He'd been all stitched up but still had to go for an MRI as he'd been knocked unconscious when he went into the pool.

Regardless of the seemingly inordinate amount of blood he'd left by the pool, the cut had been mercifully shallow and only required ten stitches. Lincoln had been faithfully by his side the whole time, holding Abraham's hand and murmuring soft words of comfort. In a prime example of just how small the world can be at times, it was Dr. Madeline Hastings who'd been the one to treat him.

"You're not having much luck of late," she remarked, upon seeing who her next patient had been.

"Yeah, not so much," mumbled Abraham.

"You really need to look after this young man of yours, Lincoln."

"Trust me, I'm wrapping him up in cotton wool as soon as we get outta here," proclaimed Lincoln.

"Sounds like it may be wise," agreed Dr. Hastings good-humoredly.

By the time Abraham had been for his MRI, which he'd passed with flying colors, and was ready to be released, quite a crowd had gathered in the waiting room – his family, Topher and Eli, Coach Whiting and the entire swim squad. Abraham walked into the waiting room to see Dr. Hastings chatting with Coach Whiting and his parents – they'd arrived when he was in the machine. Even though Abraham was in a half-groggy state due to the painkillers he noticed the look of interest that flickered between the doctor and his coach.

They'd have such beautiful babies.

The group surged forward as one, all wanting to see if he was OK. He assured them as best he could, appreciating their concern but feeling slightly overwhelmed by all the attention.

His co-captain was hanging near the back of the room and noticing his reticence, Abraham motioned for him to approach.

"Hey Abe, I'm so glad you're OK but I still feel responsible," muttered Tobias dejectedly.

"It's fine, Tobias. It was just an accident."

Tobias looked relieved but still guilty, so Abraham moved forward and gave his friend a big hug to reassure him that he was indeed forgiven.

The only real concern that Abraham had was if he'd be able to compete in the upcoming State Championships, which he demanded of the doctor when she'd finished chatting with Abraham's parents.

"You'll need to stay out of the pool for at least a week," instructed Dr. Hastings. "That's assuming you don't have any further symptoms."

"But, I ..." began Abraham.

"No arguments, Abraham," interjected Coach Whiting. "The competition is important to all of us but your health takes precedence. A shiny trophy isn't worth your life. Do you understand me?"

"Yes, Coach," agreed Abraham reluctantly.

Abraham's parents then took control of the proceedings and insisted on taking their injured son home, accompanied by Lincoln, of course. A short car ride later, they arrived home and Lincoln helped his boyfriend up the stairs and into bed, followed closely behind by the rest of the Chadwicks.

"You can stay the night with him," offered Abraham's mother.

"Thanks, Mom."

"Yes, thanks ever so much, Sheila."

"But no getting up to any mischief," instructed Burt, with a sly wink.

"Ewww," squealed Megan, who'd been hovering in the background with an aura of quiet concern.

"DAD!" grumbled Abraham, rolling his eyes at his father.

"Lighten up, Nemo. Did that knock to your head destroy your sense of humor too?"

"Don't worry, we'll be on our best behavior," promised Lincoln.

Lincoln climbed in beside Abraham fully clothed. They cuddled up in a warm cocoon of blankets. Abraham's pain medication soon saw him float off to a peaceful sleep, happy in his boyfriend's arms and content in the knowledge that he had so many people in his life who cared for him.

* * *

The next week seemed to pass excruciatingly slowly for Abraham. Dr. Hastings had recommended taking the week off from school as well, which Abraham's parents had readily agreed to and now Abraham was practically climbing the walls in frustration at being stuck at home and not being able to swim. Fortunately, the near constant tender affection and consoling embrace of his boyfriend helped to soothe his frayed nerves. He'd had a few slight headaches since the accident but Abraham had been told to expect that and as long as they didn't increase in intensity or frequency there was nothing to be concerned about.

At the end of the week, Abraham received some wonderful news, as Lincoln was finally off the waiting list to Port Davinica

University and accepted into their drama program for the coming academic year. Strangely, Abraham detected a slight note of reservation in his boyfriend's tone when he'd told him about the acceptance letter.

"You don't look as happy as I thought you'd be. Don't you want to go there any more?" inquired Abraham.

"Yeah, I do…it's just…I've been thinking 'bout maybe having a year off."

"Oh? But what would you do? Get a job?"

"Well, I was thinking 'bout going to Europe for a while."

Abraham was flabbergasted. Lincoln hadn't mentioned anything about traveling before and Abraham's mind spun with questions, which then battled to make it out of his mouth all at once.

"For how long? By yourself? How can you afford that?" Abraham's voice became increasingly shrill with worry.

"Hey, Beau, calm down. Nothing's set. I'm not sure how long it would be for, but I was going to ask ya to come with me. I hadn't said anything because I was waiting for ya to be all better. Think about it. It could be really great, exploring all those different countries and cultures together…and all the mischief we could get up to."

"Yeah, I guess." His response was less than enthusiastic. "I just hadn't thought about doing anything else except college."

Lincoln took Abraham's hand in his and looked him in the eyes with an indulgent gaze.

"We don't need to decide anything now. I wanted to keep my options open is all. We OK?"

"Of course…you just caught me by surprise. I was worried that I was already losing you."

Abraham looked away, ashamed of sounding so needy. The unexpected news and accompanying swell of worry and doubt had thrown his heart into turmoil.

Ergh, I sound pathetic.

"Losing me? I promise, Beau, you're far too precious to me for that to ever happen."

Lifting his face towards Lincoln, Abraham saw nothing but love and kindness in his boyfriend's eyes. While he felt slightly more reassured, Abraham was still left with an uneasy feeling about what the future may bring them.

Could I be away for a whole year?

* * *

Abraham was in the midst of having an exceptionally good day. He'd been back in the pool for a week and his times didn't seem to have been affected by his week off. If anything they'd slightly improved, the rest apparently having done his body a world of good. To top it off, today was his birthday! He had awoken to a singing phone call from Lincoln, followed shortly afterwards by several congratulatory messages and texts from his friends, all making him feel very loved indeed. While Abraham was still lazing in bed, his parents had brought up his presents – mostly clothes and swimming paraphernalia – and his favorite breakfast – blueberry pancakes with a side of crispy bacon and smothered in maple syrup.

After swim practice, Topher had walked with Abraham down to the bleachers as they were supposed to meet up with

Lincoln and Eli to all go out for dinner in honor of his birthday. When they arrived at the field, however, all the lighting had been turned off and the place appeared deserted and ominously dark. A sudden shiver snaked down Abraham's spine and he felt quite vulnerable.

"Where is everyone? This is the when the serial killer jumps out and hacks us to pieces," joked Abraham, trying to shake his unnerving sensation of impending doom.

"Not tonight," countered Topher with a mischievous smile that Abraham knew all too well.

"What are you guys up…"

Just then the speakers burst into life with the strains of Happy Birthday. A light came on by the end of the field, highlighting Lincoln standing by the goal posts.

What's he up to?

Abraham smiled widely at his boyfriend, his mind burning with curiosity. The music suddenly changed and became much more dancey and electronic. Abraham could see shadowy figures moving randomly about the field. Suddenly all the lights came up and he could see that the entire cheer squad was there, complete with the mascot.

Absolutely stunned, Abraham's mouth dropped open as the squad proceeded to launch into a spectacular dance routine with tumbles, jumps, cartwheels and somersaults. It seemed even more elaborate than their usual football routines and Abraham still wasn't completely sure what was going on. He kept looking to Topher for some sort of guidance but his best friend merely grinned and kept directing Abraham's gaze back to the spectacle before them.

After a few minutes the routine came to a rousing finish with several cheerleaders being thrown into the air and Lincoln ending up on bended knee in the grass right in front of Abraham.

"Abraham Chadwick, will ya do me the honor of accompanying me to the prom?"

A promposal? This only happens in unrealistic teen movies.

"I don't know…I'll have to think about it." He paused long enough for Lincoln's confident smile to falter slightly. "Of course I will, Linc!"

As the pair embraced and kissed, there were many cheers of 'Happy Birthday' and 'Congratulations' from the assembled crowd, who were clearly pleased that their efforts hadn't been in vain. The group slowly broke up and accompanied by Lincoln, Topher and Eli, Abraham headed off to his favorite restaurant – The Flaming Sombrero – where they served the hottest Mexican food in the city. Their chicken nachos always succeeded in making Abraham sweat and cry with his nose running all at the same time – he loved it! Lincoln wasn't opposed to the odd spiciness from time to time but he was nowhere near as big a chili-head as his boyfriend.

Abraham could barely believe that his life was going so well. Six months ago, the idea of dating a hot cheerleader and being asked to prom in such a fantastic fashion would have seemed like total science fiction.

Now if we could only find the right time to fuck.

* * *

A few days later, Abraham, Lincoln and Topher were

standing in line at Geek HQ, patiently waiting to get their Blue Hunter comics signed by their creator Timothy Waters. Lincoln had turned Abraham onto the series of graphic novels, about a leather-clad vigilante and his steadfast sidekick, not long after they'd started dating and had given him the complete series for his birthday. Abraham had gotten Topher hooked as well, not surprising given their geeky natures and the numerous explicit scenes of superhero sexploits depicted within each issue. It would be fair to say that the comics had inspired a good deal of self-pleasuring for the trio…and a great many others judging by the length of the queue.

There were a few other artists signing in-store today but the line for Blue Hunter was easily the longest. It undoubtedly helped that the graphic artist had quite prepossessing features – intelligent hazel eyes, chestnut-brown hair, a sparkling smile and a solid build that filled out his Blue Hunter t-shirt and snug jeans very nicely. Naturally, the queue was heavy with gentleman of a certain persuasion but there were a few ladies in attendance that obviously enjoyed the overt displays of male loving that appeared in amongst the brightly colored pages.

"Damn, I didn't know he was so hot," remarked Topher, after he'd caught sight of the artist.

"Down, boy," teased Abraham. "What if Eli heard you? Isn't he supposed to be here already?"

"He'd probably say the same thing and yeah he was coming right here after Cassidy helped him dye his hair."

The hue of Eli's hair changed on a regular basis, having gone through the spectrum of the rainbow a few times over, much to his mother's mortification. To tell the truth Abraham was a little envious of Eli's devil-may-care attitude when it came to his appearance. He secretly wished he was brave enough to shake things up, although given Lincoln's many compliments about his auburn locks, Abraham was unlikely to do anything drastic to them in the near future.

"What color this time?" queried Abraham.

"He wouldn't tell me...wanted it to be a surprise."

They shuffled forward as the queue moved along closer to the table. Lincoln winced in pain when he moved his right leg, as he'd rolled his ankle at cheer practice the night before.

"You, OK?" asked Abraham, his voice conveying his loving concern.

"Yeah, it's just a little sore."

"I'd carry you if I could."

"That's awfully generous of ya, kind Sir, but I think I'll be fine and dandy by tomorrow." Lincoln gave Abraham a quick peck on the lips. "Topher's right though. The guy is fine," added Lincoln.

"You can settle down too," smirked Abraham.

"Awww, but you know I only really have eyes for ya, Beau."

"Hand me a bucket," joked Topher.

"Hey, you and Eli were far worse when you first got together."

"I have no memory of what you're talking about." Topher poked out his tongue. "Besides, if we did it, it would have been hot."

Just then Eli arrived, his hair lucent with vibrant shades of blue. He walked over to the trio and gave Topher a very friendly kiss, which began to border on indecent.

"Hey guys," greeted Eli warmly, when he managed to break free of the fierce lip-lock. "So what do you think of the new color?"

"We certainly won't lose you," teased Lincoln.

"Looks good," remarked Abraham.

"Another triumph, my love," praised Topher.

Seemingly pleased with the reaction, Eli looked down the length of the queue towards the signing table.

"Damn, that author guy's hot; maybe I need to get more into comics."

Topher let out a little chuckle and gave Abraham a smug smile to which Abraham simply shook his head. The incident in the mountains hadn't appeared to dampen either of their flirty natures.

"What did I miss?" Eli looked puzzled.

The trio just laughed lightheartedly, only adding to Eli's confusion.

"Nothing, babe," said Topher, giving Eli an affectionate hug.

Abraham smiled looking at the pair of them. He was glad to no longer feel like an outsider when it came to love and relationships.

"What you grinning about?" asked Lincoln.

"Just happy."

"Good. That makes me happy too, Beau."

Lincoln reached his strong arms out and brought Abraham into a tight embrace. Abraham inhaled deeply, soaking up the familiar, fiercely masculine scent of his loving boyfriend.

* * *

Standing on the podium beside Tobias, Julie and Sarah – the co-captains of the girls' swim squad – Abraham had never felt prouder. The last week of intensive training had paid off and together the foursome had just won the mixed-medley relay. Abraham's body was tingling with excitement as the crowd clapped and cheered around them, while the small gold medals were placed around their necks and they each took a turn holding up the trophy. Abraham could see his family, Lincoln and a good many of his classmates in the audience applauding their success. The State Championships had been held in Port Davinica this year, at the university pool, the previous year's winners always assumed the right to host the competition.

A few hours later, Abraham and the rest of the swim squad members were still the center of attention at the victory party being held at Julie and Jonas' family home – a sprawling five-bedroom house at the edge of the city. The place was soon packed to bursting with what looked like the entire senior class and a good chunk of the juniors as well. Some parents had made a brief appearance, as well as Coach Whiting, but none had stayed very long, not wanting to hamper the youngsters' fun. Lincoln stayed steadfastly by Abraham's side for most of the night and the lads were being especially affectionate towards one another.

"The only thing that could make tonight better…" whispered Abraham.

"I know," Lincoln replied, his eyes twinkling. "Soon, Beau. Soon."

Everyone was in a celebratory mood and Abraham was enjoying himself immensely. He felt like a mini-celebrity, as he received hugs and high-fives from a seemingly unending swarm of adoring fans. The numerous celebratory drinks that had been handed to him throughout the evening warmed him and made his head begin to swim a little. After a few hours, the ice supplies had started to run low so Lincoln and Tobias had volunteered to fetch some more.

"You sure you don't want me to come with you?" asked Abraham.

"Nah, stay and bask in the glory. I'll be back before ya know it."

Lincoln gave Abraham a soft peck on the lips and headed out, leaving Abraham to continue soaking up the praise.

A short while later, Abraham stood up to go the bathroom but felt dreadfully unsteady on his feet. He didn't think that he'd had that much to drink but he hadn't really been keeping track. Fortunately, he was able to slowly make his way to the bathroom without incident but after he'd finished he started to become quite disorientated. As he exited the bathroom, Abraham stumbled and almost fell but was caught by a large pair of hands and helped to his feet.

"Hey Swim Champ, you OK?" asked Jonas.

"Yeah, just had too much to drink, I guess," slurred Abraham.

"Do you want to rest upstairs for a bit?"

"I don't know…Lincoln will be back…I don't…"

He trailed off as his mind became even fuzzier. The noises of the party seemed muffled and Abraham had the impression of trying to move under water.

"You can sleep it off in my room. I'll let Lincoln know where you are when he gets back," offered Jonas.

"OK…I should probably lay…thanks," mumbled Abraham, glad that someone was helping him.

"No problemo, buddy."

They made their way upstairs with Abraham leaning heavily on Jonas for support. They entered the bedroom, which was dimly lit by a lamp in the far corner.

"You're sure…" started Abraham, struggling to focus.

"Yup. Just take it easy."

"Don't forget to tell Lincoln…to tell…"

Abraham collapsed onto the bed and the room began to spin. His eyes felt so heavy, but he was reluctant to close them, as he didn't want to fall asleep.

Maybe just for a minute or two.

The next thing Abraham knew the room seemed to be full of furious voices. He blearily opened his eyes and saw a very angry-looking Lincoln standing by the bed and yelling.

"What the FUCK is going on?"

"Lincoln?" asked Abraham groggily.

"Answer me, Abe!" demanded Lincoln irately.

"Just relax, we were only having a little fun," smirked Jonas.

It was then that Abraham's mind cleared enough to realize the gravity of the situation. He was in bed with Jonas! And when Abraham quickly placed his hand under the covers he discovered an even worse predicament – he was bare-ass naked.

What have I done?

"Ya weren't ready for me but you let *him* fuck ya?" interrogated Lincoln, his face full of fury.

"No, I… I don't know…I don't remember." Abraham tried to explain but was struggling with his foggy brain.

"UNBELIEVABLE! I've been looking for ya for an hour and you've been here the whole time? How could ya do this, I thought ya loved me?"

Lincoln furiously rushed from the room. Abraham had never seen him look so angry or hurt.

I've got to go after him!

"What a drama queen," remarked Jonas snarkily.

"Shut up, Jonas! Where the fuck are my clothes?" growled Abraham, his own rage barely contained.

"On the floor where you left them."

"What did you do to me?"

"Nothing! You were the one who came on to me. Begging me to fuck you…so I did. You weren't half bad."

The world seemed to fall out from under Abraham. To lose his virginity and have no memory of it was one thing, but to do so while cheating on his boyfriend was even worse.

This can't be happening!

He hurriedly dressed himself and rushed outside to find Lincoln but ran straight into Topher instead.

"Dude, what's going on? I just saw Lincoln screech out of here looking like Hell."

"I've fucked everything up!" cried Abraham.

"Hey, calm down. What's happened?" asked Topher.

"I don't know…I…what have I done?"

Abraham fell into Topher's arms sobbing and completely bewildered as to how this could have happened to him. Topher messaged Eli to meet them out the front and together they drove Abraham, who had fallen into a silent, almost fugue-like state, back home.

"I think I have to stay with him tonight," said Topher.

"Do you want me to stay too?" asked Eli gently.

"Nah, I got this. Call you tomorrow," replied Topher with a sad smile.

They kissed each other goodbye and Topher led Abraham up to his bedroom and did his best to comfort his distraught friend.

* * *

The next morning Abraham and Topher were sitting in Abraham's bedroom trying to work out what exactly had happened at the party. Abraham had been crying off and on ever since he'd gotten home the previous night and the two of them had only had a few hours of broken sleep. It didn't help that Abraham felt extremely hung over – tired, nauseous and with a huge gap in his memory.

"How could I be so stupid? What was I thinking? I don't even remember what happened," lamented Abraham once more, pacing the room fitfully, unable to keep still.

"You need to calm down, Abe. You'll make yourself sick."

Topher had been trying in vain for most of the night to pacify Abraham's agitated state.

"How can I? I have no idea what I did and I've probably lost my boyfriend forever. I wouldn't blame him for hating me. I hate me! I've been trying so hard to remember but I just keep drawing a blank."

"That's what's so weird. You've never blacked out like that before and from what I saw you weren't drinking any more than usual."

"Do you think I could have been affected by the endorphins in my system from the win?" asked Abraham, in an increasingly desperate attempt to explain his behavior.

"Maybe."

Topher didn't look or sound particularly convinced, although Abraham could practically see the wheels turning behind his eyes about something.

"What are you thinking?" inquired Abraham.

"I'm not sure…only that it just doesn't seem to make sense."

"Tell me about it! I hold out to lose my virginity to someone I love so it would be special and memorable… like with you and Eli. Then I go and lose it to *Jonas* of all people and I can't recall a damn thing!"

"You've got to go easier on yourself," placated Topher.

"Why? I deserve everything that's coming to me. I fucked up and I have no one to blame but myself."

"I'm not so sure about that."

Abraham stopped dead still, interrupting his frantic pacing. There was something in Topher's tone of voice that gave him hope.

"What do you mean? What do you think happened?"

"I don't know for sure but I have a vague idea…I don't want to say any more until I check a few things out, but I don't think that you're to blame…well not entirely."

The brief hope that Abraham was clinging to flickered and faded away, as he assumed that it was only a misguided attempt on Topher's behalf to make him feel better.

"Thanks for trying to cheer me up but it *is* all my fault. I kinda feel like wallowing a bit. Do you mind if I spend some time alone?"

"You sure?" questioned Topher, clearly unwilling to leave his distraught best friend all by himself.

"Yeah, I'll call you later. I just need some time to process and work out what I'm going to do next."

"OK, but if I don't hear from you soon, I'll be back banging on your door and dragging you back into the real world."

"And I appreciate it."

"You'll get through this, I promise."

They came together in a strong, warm hug, which they held for a good minute. Immediately after Topher left, Abraham dived back into his bed, pulled the covers over his head and started to softly weep.

I just want to die!

* * *

Abraham had spent the whole weekend crying and sporadically trying to contact Lincoln, neither having any sort of positive effect. Lincoln was most definitely ignoring his calls and messages; Abraham would've even tried a carrier pigeon if he thought it would elicit a response. He was too afraid to go to Lincoln's house, terrified at the thought of no longer seeing any love in his boyfriend's eyes.

That Monday, Abraham dreaded going to school as he could only imagine the rumors flying about the place since his very public fight at the party. To make matters worse, the stress had caused an unsightly rash to breakout on the side of his neck and shoulders. Abraham forced himself to get dressed and catch a lift with Topher, as he knew he had to confront the issue at some point. Plus, if there was a chance of hopefully salvaging his relationship, he needed to apologize to Lincoln in person.

"It'll be OK," said Topher encouragingly, as they walked into the side entrance from the car park.

Abraham gave only a thin-lipped smile in return and bravely continued forward. Throughout the morning, Abraham noticed people looking at him oddly and speaking in hushed tones when he neared, confirming that the whole school already knew what had happened.

If only I could remember.

It was halfway through the day before Abraham had his chance to speak with Lincoln. Just after lunch he was walking towards his next class – biology – where they would definitely see each other. Abraham was nearly at the lab when he saw Lincoln standing by the lockers talking to Austin. His heart caught in his throat and he stopped walking, feeling as if he was glued to the spot in fear and shame.

Go talk to him! I can't, he probably hates me. I won't know if I don't try.

He forced himself to move and was about two feet away when Lincoln suddenly turned to face him with a look of surprise. Abraham could also see a dark look of disdain on Austin's face.

OK, so he hates me too.

Abraham wasn't too surprised but it still hurt nevertheless. It was the expression on Lincoln's face, however, that cut straight to Abraham's heart and stopped him midstride. In his eyes there wasn't anger, only a deep disappointment and sadness. Lincoln just shook his head and slowly turned away.

"You've got some nerve," snarled Austin, in a far more aggressive tone than Abraham had ever heard from him, before he too turned away.

After the awkward encounter, Abraham felt sick to his stomach. He went to the school nurse, a non-descript woman in her late sixties, who mistook his pale countenance and rash for illness and sent him home to recover.

"You poor love, feel better soon," said Nurse Church kindly.

He felt even guiltier about lying but he couldn't bear to be at school any more. Abraham went home and spent the next few days in his room listening to his favorite sad song – Youth by Daughter – on repeat and wallowing in his misery, with Captain Reynolds curled up faithfully by his side. His parents were understandably concerned and checked on him periodically but didn't want to pry too much into what had happened. They did leave plates of food by his door and encouraged him to come downstairs all to no avail.

Abraham had received messages from friends wanting to know if he was OK but he just couldn't face the world again at the moment. The only visitor he would consent to seeing was Topher, who despite his best efforts couldn't raise Abraham out of his deep well of sadness and self-pity.

I deserve this! I'm pathetic and will end up all alone!

* * *

After five days of his self-imposed exile, Abraham managed to leave his room. The bright sunshine streaming in through his bedroom window had lifted his spirits slightly, so he changed into his swimwear, went downstairs and plunged into the pool.

Captain Reynolds also appeared happy to be out in the sunshine once more, as he'd spent the last week inside attempting to provide comfort to his morose owner.

Swimming had always soothed his mind in the past but he hadn't felt like getting in the water since the incident at the party. As his body fell into the comforting rhythm of slicing through the water, Abraham felt the tension and sadness begin to ease. The water was refreshing on the unseasonably hot spring day and Abraham soon felt refreshed and revitalized. After he completed thirty laps, Abraham was fatigued but felt much clearer-headed and more in control of his emotions. He was toweling off on the patio when he heard voices coming through the thick hedge that separated his yard from his neighbors behind – the Deacons.

He wandered over to the side of the hedge and peeked through. There, on the sun lounges by the pool, Abraham saw Simon Deacon's brother – and Abraham's favorite underwear model – Ali, getting lotion rubbed on his back by a tall, sturdy hunk of muscle. Both men were sporting almost indecently skimpy swimwear from the latest CocKed summer range – Abraham practically memorized each catalogue. He could only see the duo in profile, but there was something familiar about the other man that stirred a memory.

Where have I seen him before?

The rubbing started to get more sensual and soon the pair began kissing ardently. Unsurprisingly, Abraham's member started to stir in his navy-blue swimmers, awakened by the sizzling scene unfolding before him. His body couldn't help it, he'd been too depressed to pleasure himself in nearly a week and his un-sated desires took control. Moving forward to get a better look, Abraham broke a branch and attracted their attention. Abraham tried to move fully back into his yard but his towel was snagged on the hedge and he was stuck.

"Who's there?" asked the stranger, in a deep baritone that Abraham recognized straight away.

No, it can't be! Officer Ford?

"What are you doing there, you little pervert?" demanded Officer Ford, as he approached the hedge.

"I'm...I'm sorry... I heard voices...then I couldn't stop watching...I'm sorry...I just..."

"Brad, relax, it's just the neighbor kid," said Ali, as he moved over to join them, his dark chest hair glistening with sun lotion.

Officer Ford grabbed a hold of Abraham's arm and pulled him forward, he soon came free on the hedge and half stumbled into the Deacons' backyard. His towel had stuck fast to the hedge, leaving Abraham standing there in his Speedos, his erection appearing dangerously close to bursting forth at any moment.

"Doesn't look like a kid to me," barked Officer Ford, as he took in the sight of Abraham.

"Damn! You're right about that. So you liked what you saw, handsome? Wanna have some fun?" offered Ali, emanating an intoxicating air of mischief.

Abraham had to admit that despite everything he found the offer tempting. In fact, pre-Lincoln it would have been a wet dream come true. After all, he'd already had multiple fantasies about Ali – not to mention that the idea of playing with a real-live cop was ridiculously hot – but when his cock stopped thinking his heart chimed back in.

"Give it a rest, Ali," Officer Ford, although there was good humor in the timbre of his voice. "What's your name, son?"

"Abe."

"Hold on a sec, don't I know you? Yeah...I caught you and your boy messing around in a jeep up at The Head, didn't I?"

"Yes, Sir," admitted Abraham feeling terribly embarrassed.

"You stopped them fucking? You're such a spoilsport," taunted Ali.

"Hey, the law isn't up to me. Personally, I don't care where people fuck but I had a job to do. So, what were you doing spying on us when you've got a young man of your own?"

The mention of his missing boyfriend stirred up Abraham's already turbulent emotions and he soon found himself on the verge of tears. His eyes shimmered, as the sorrow inside fought to be released.

"Hey, Abe, it's OK. I'm sorry if I was rough on you," said Officer Ford, the timbre of his voice becoming much more sympathetic.

"No... it's not that. It's...It's...It's Lincoln. I've lost him and don't think I'll ever get him back," cried Abraham, hot tears starting to roll down his face.

Officer Ford took the weeping Abraham by the hand, led him over to the sun lounge and sat him down. Ali and Officer Ford sat either side of Abraham, trying to calm him down.

"OK, no need for all those tears, now."

"Why don't you tell us all about it?"

And so, to his great surprise, Abraham found himself repeating the whole sorry tale to his new acquaintances. They listened quietly, as Abraham recounted his greatest shame and then hastened to reassure him from their collective experience with affairs of the heart.

"You just have to give him time. It's only been a week and it sounds like it was a pretty big deal for both of you," counseled Ali.

"Giving him space is good, but don't leave it too long," cautioned Officer Ford. "If you truly love the guy then you need to fight for the relationship before he has a chance to move on."

"Thanks guys. This has really helped." Abraham was indeed feeling calmer and somewhat more reassured. "Sorry for perving on you."

"No problem at all. I take it as a compliment," remarked Ali proudly.

"Of course, *you* would," scoffed Officer Ford.

"Thanks, guys I really appreciate you listening to me."

"Our pleasure," beamed Ali.

"Hope it works out," added Officer Ford.

Abraham bid them farewell and squeezed his way back through the hedge, retrieving his towel on the way. Never in his wildest fantasies could he have anticipated that he'd spend the afternoon getting relationship advice from his favorite underwear model and a brawny cop but Abraham had to admit that he felt a lot better for it. He also had a much more hopeful outlook for his future with Lincoln.

Maybe there's still a chance.

* * *

The following evening, Abraham had another surprising conversation. He had returned to school that day but Lincoln hadn't been there. Consequently, he'd come home in a miserable mood, convinced that Lincoln had taken the day off to avoid him. All the optimism he'd built up after chatting with Ali and Brad the day before had crumbled away. He was sulking in his room when there was a light tapping on his door.

"Abe, it's me can I come in?" Megan's soft, muffled voice came through the door.

"No!"

Abraham wasn't feeling in the mood to deal with anyone, let alone his kid sister.

Why can't everyone just leave me alone!

"Please, Abe. I want to talk to you."

Abraham relented, partly because he feared she would go running off to their parents and get him into trouble if he refused to see her.

"OK, come in," agreed Abraham with a resigned air.

Tentatively, Megan opened the door and came into the room. She surveyed the mess covering just about every surface, apparently in search for somewhere to sit, and wrinkled her face in concern – Abraham's room was normally the very picture of neatness. Walking over to the desk, Megan cleared the crumpled clothes off of the chair and sat down.

"Well?" demanded Abraham impatiently.

"Your room is…"

"It's what?" Abraham's temper was beginning to bubble. "If you just wanted to come in here and criticize me then you can get out, now!"

"I…I wanted to see how you were doing, you big jerk."

"I'm fine. Anything else?"

"No…and no you're not fine. I may be younger than you but I'm not an idiot. I guess it's to do with Lincoln, but mom and dad won't tell me anything either. I can tell they're worried and so am I. Please, Abe, won't you talk to me about it?"

"I'll be fine," said Abraham gruffly.

"It's just that you were so happy before and it was good to see you smiling all the time. You were nicer to be around and now you seem so *miserable*. I know we don't always get along but you're my brother and I love you. I just want you to be happy."

Moved by Megan's unexpected show of compassion and concern, Abraham felt the shell he'd constructed around himself start to crack.

It can't hurt to tell her a little.

"It's my own fault. I made a stupid mistake and I ruined things with Lincoln," admitted Abraham desolately.

"I don't think so," replied Megan, a look of determination fixed on her visage.

"What?"

"Whatever it is I'm sure you two can work it out."

She doesn't know what I did. It was unforgivable.

"I just don't think we will, Monkey."

It was nickname he hadn't used for years and Abraham saw Megan's face light up at the sound of it. It seemed as if the closeness of their childhood might not have been quite as lost as Abraham had thought.

"I don't think you've lost him forever. I saw the way you looked at each other," exclaimed Megan, her eyes full of hope.

She watches too many soap operas.

"Thanks, but…"

"No buts! I really think you guys are made for each other. Don't give up, OK?"

"I'll try," promised Abraham, with as much enthusiasm as he could muster.

"That's all I ask. OK, gotta go. Teen Wolf is on."

And with that she flounced out of the room and downstairs to watch her favorite program – well, for this week anyway. Left by himself, Abraham pondered her words.

Maybe she's right.

A small smile crossed Abraham's face at the thought of taking advice from his baby sister, who appeared to be growing up faster than he cared to admit. The pep talk was exactly what Abraham needed to restore his confidence and he resolved not to give up on his relationship with Lincoln just yet.

I'll try again tomorrow!

* * *

The next day Abraham awoke with his determined attitude intact. His dreams had been full of happy, nonsensical adventures with Lincoln by his side, and it made Abraham even more resolute to try and salvage his relationship.

If he's not at school, I'll go to his house and I'll make him listen to me!

He arrived at school with a single-minded purpose but was soon waylaid by Topher, who grabbed Abraham when he was opening his locker.

"You have to meet me in the band room right after third period," commanded Topher.

"I can't. That's Lincoln' free period and I need to talk to him."

"That's perfect. Come to the band room then and everything will work itself out."

"What do you mean?" inquired Abraham his interest peaked.

"Do you trust me?"

"Yes, you know I do but I really don't under…"

"Just promise me you'll meet me there."

There was a seriousness to Topher that Abraham hadn't seen for quite a long time. Realizing there was no arguing with his best friend, Abraham reluctantly agreed.

"OK, I'll see you then."

Topher rushed off, leaving Abraham to make his way to French class, his curiosity burning bright.

Could everything turn out all right? But I don't see how Topher can fix everything.

The first two periods seemed to drag with an agonizing sluggishness, all the while Abraham was torturing himself with what he was going to say to Lincoln to try and make things right. Finally, the bell rang throughout the school and Abraham rushed to the band room, only to find it completely deserted. He sat down on one of the wooden chairs and looked nervously around the room. The chairs and music stands had been pushed to the side leaving the space wide open – it was also one of the places the Glee club rehearsed and the room had been undoubtedly cleared for them. Abraham had been to a couple of rehearsals to watch Lincoln singing and dancing away with the group. The memory of it made him start to tear up slightly.

What if I can't get him back?

Just then the door swung open and in walked Lincoln. He scanned the room and saw Abraham, his face changing into a palpable picture of sadness. Abraham could see that the look of disappointment in his eyes hadn't diminished, although this time there was a fair amount of anger mixed into it as well.

"Topher told me to meet him here," explained Lincoln, clearly wishing to be anywhere else.

"He told me the same thing. I…"

"Abe, I don't want to hear it."

The harsh timbre of Lincoln's voice tore at Abraham's heart, enflaming the open wound. Abraham hadn't thought he could feel any worse but the animosity coming from his boyfriend was excruciating. Even so, Abraham couldn't give up his quest.

"Please, I need to try and exp…"

"I can't…I can't forgive ya. I'm sorry, Abe, but it's over."

The words shook Abraham to his core, leaving him at a complete loss, watching silently as Lincoln turned to walk out of the room. Before he reached the door, Topher barged into the music room with a very sorry-looking Jonas trailing behind him.

"What the fuck is he doing here?" growled Lincoln, his body bristling with rage.

"Please, just calm down," pleaded Topher.

"I can't deal with this, I'm out of here!" shouted Lincoln.

"Topher, what the hell are you doing?" demanded Abraham.

"Lincoln, wait! You both need to hear what Jonas has to say."

"I don't care what this asshole has to say," grumbled Lincoln through gritted teeth.

"Neither do I," agreed Abraham vehemently.

Topher stepped in front of the door to prevent either of them from leaving.

"Trust me! You both need to listen, if you want to know the truth about what went on at Jonas' party.

"I KNOW ENOUGH!" yelled Lincoln.

"NO...you don't. Now sit your asses down and listen. If you want to storm out after that's fine but you need to know what actually happened."

Topher's brand new authoritative tone surprised and subdued the pair so they begrudgingly sat down. The tension in the room was unnervingly thick and discomfiting. Meanwhile, Jonas was standing by the wall looking more and more uncomfortable.

"Jonas, tell them," commanded Topher.

"I...it wasn't...Abe didn't..." stammered Jonas.

"Spit it out!" commanded Lincoln.

"It was all me! Abe didn't do a damn thing."

The room went deathly silent as the unexpected confession hung in the air. Hope began to flicker inside Abraham's heart.

It wasn't my fault?

"What *exactly* do ya mean?" demanded Lincoln.

"I was kinda pissed after you both turned me down, so I thought that I'd get a little payback...I slipped something in Abe's drink."

"YOU WHAT?" screamed Abraham.

A maelstrom of emotion surged through Abraham, as anger, shock and disbelief struggled for dominance. He honestly didn't know whether to cry, yell or laugh.

"It was just a few of my mom's Ambien. Just enough to knock him out and then I stripped him down and hopped into bed with him so it would look like we fucked. I didn't do anything to him...I like my playmates to play back." Jonas half-laughed but evidently sensing the increasingly dangerous mood, he continued his explanation. "I'm *really* sorry, I didn't think it would go this far but then when it all blew up it was too late."

"Why are you confessing now?" demanded Abraham, still struggling to process the revelation.

"Because Topher worked it out and threatened to go to the police if I didn't admit to what I'd done. I'm sorry guys, I didn't think it through."

"So you and I never had sex?" asked Abraham, desperately wanting to confirm this new series of events.

"No...well I might have groped you a little but..."

All of a sudden, Lincoln leaped from his chair and pinned Jonas to the ground.

"You fucking asshole! You're going to pay for what you did!"

Topher and Abraham quickly jumped up and, with quite some difficulty, pulled Lincoln off of Jonas. He struggled in their arms for a good minute before beginning to calm down again. When the fury had faded enough, for rational thought to resume, Lincoln turned to Abraham, his countenance awash with shame.

"Beau, I'm *so* sorry. I'm sorry I didn't have faith in you. Can you ever forgive me?" begged Lincoln.

While he was still hurt that Lincoln had so quickly abandoned him, Abraham knew full well that if the situation were reversed he most likely would have behaved in exactly the same manner. Taking a mature stance, Abraham decided to lay the upset and recriminations where they truly belonged – on Jonas.

"How could you trust me when I didn't even know what I'd done? I didn't even have any faith in myself," admitted Abraham. "I don't blame you."

"You're sure, Beau?"

Abraham could see the hopefulness and love in Lincoln's eyes and knew he'd made the right decision.

"How about we both agree to move on together?"

"Done!" exclaimed Lincoln, happiness beaming from his every fiber.

The boys lovingly embraced, while Topher looked on with smug satisfaction. Jonas, who had since gotten back on his feet, was slowly backing out of the room. As he reached the door, Jonas turned and interrupted the boys' heartfelt reunion.

"I'm really sorry, guys...so, we're good?"

Abraham turned to look at Jonas. Without saying a word, Abraham calmly walked over towards the quarterback and punched him square in the face, knocking him back down to the ground.

"We're not even close to *good*!" declared Abraham.

Jonas was curled up on the floor, his hand cupped around his rapidly swelling nose. A small trail of blood was trickling from his left nostril. It gave Abraham a wonderful sense of satisfaction.

"Fuck! Fuck, fuck, fuck. I think you broke my nose, Abe," whimpered Jonas.

"Good, maybe next time you'll think twice about drugging someone."

Jonas struggled to his feet again and rushed out of the room, making his escape without a backward glance.

"That felt great! Although my hand's a bit sore." Abraham nursed his injured fist but with a happy expression. "I owe you big time, Topher."

"What are best friends for, if not for exposing nefarious schemes?" quipped Topher.

"Topher, how can I ever repay you?" asked Lincoln, his voice wavering with emotion.

"You can start by giving your boyfriend a big kiss."

"My pleasure."

Lincoln swept Abraham up into his arms and gave him the longest, most passionate kiss that they had ever shared. Topher smiled and quietly exited the room, leaving the reunited couple in peace. When they finally broke apart, both had matching grins and radiated an aura of pure joy.

"I'm so sorry…" began Lincoln, attempting to apologize again.

"Shhh…I just want to go back how we were before."

"But what about Jonas? We can't just let him get away with this!" insisted Lincoln.

A swell of irritation coursed through Abraham at the thought of the quarterback's malicious actions, causing his body to tense up and his smile begin to fade.

"I can't think about him right now. He's already cost us so much time apart and worry. Can we please just focus on us, for now?"

"Your wish is my command, Beau."

They came together again, their bodies entwined as one, kissing and holding each other for quite some time, only breaking apart when the bell rang at the end of the period.

* * *

Finally, after what seemed like months of waiting, the night of the senior prom had arrived. It was to be an extra special night for Abraham and Lincoln, as another long wait was about to be over for them as well. After their first two failed attempts, nothing short of a crashing meteorite was going to interfere with their plans – third time's the charm!

Together, along with the rest of the senior class, the lads were seated in the main ballroom of the Grand Babylon Hotel. The room had been tastefully decorated in shades of black and gold, in accordance with the Roaring Twenties theme – feathers, cocktail glasses and tassels abounded…very Gatsby-esque, indeed.

The boys made quite the handsome couple in their midnight-black, bespoke suits, which they'd had fashioned at A Gentlemanly Touch in the city. In fact, a great many of the guys in their year had done the same – due to the tailor's sterling reputation. Mr. Applewhite, the seamster in question, was rather nimble of finger, as well as being extraordinarily talented, and their suits had been ready a mere two weeks after their first fitting. The outfits were completed with sharp white shirts, matching electric-blue pocket-handkerchiefs and ties, and shiny black dress shoes. Their parents had made an embarrassing fuss of taking photos and getting a tad weepy before they'd been allowed to leave in the limo they'd hired together with Topher and Eli.

The foursome was sitting together, along with Tobias, Lydia, Austin and Cassidy, at a large, round, linen-covered table, finishing up their light supper before the dancing was to begin. Abraham's gaze was drawn to the far table by the exit where Jonas was sitting awkwardly alone and looking thoroughly miserable. His two black eyes had all but faded away and his nose had reduced back to its normal size, fortunately it hadn't been broken.

People had been treating Jonas as a pariah over the past month, even Penny had refused to speak with him any longer. Abraham was a tad surprised that the quarterback had even come to the dance. Neither Abraham nor Lincoln had talked particularly openly about what had happened, but the rumor mill had filled in the blanks and the whole school now knew about that fateful night – or a variation of it at least. Regardless, everyone seemed to get the gist that Jonas was the villain of the piece and had nearly succeeded in breaking up one of the most popular senior couples.

"I still can't believe he had the balls to show up," commented Lincoln gruffly, after noticing where Abraham was looking.

"Well it's his prom too. Just try and ignore him," implored Abraham softly.

"I still think ya should have gone to the police."

It remained a small sticking point between the couple that Abraham hadn't pursued the matter further. Lincoln had, however, begrudgingly agreed not to take his own revenge out on the quarterback.

"Let's just enjoy our evening," stated Abraham firmly.

"Why, of course, Beau," said Lincoln, adopting his overly polite persona. "Would ya like me to fetch ya a refreshment?"

"Thank you, kind Sir. I am feeling ever so parched," cooed Abraham, doing his very best Southern Belle impression.

They smiled at one another, the tension between them eased. Abraham then watched with a loving regard as Lincoln walked over to the bar in the corner. Coming to a decision, Abraham abruptly got up from the table.

"Where are you going, Abe?" questioned Topher.

"There's something I need to do."

Abraham walked determinedly across the room and came to a stop in front of Jonas, who looked up in surprise.

"You're not going to hit me again are you?" asked Jonas a tad fearfully.

"No, and…I'm sorry about what I did to your face."

"Don't be. I deserved if for dosing you and almost ruining your relationship…I've done a lot of soul searching about what I did and how I've been acting towards people. I'm trying to change."

"I'm glad to hear it," remarked Abraham genuinely.

"Everyone thinks I'm evil. I don't even know why I came tonight."

Abraham could practically see the black cloud of melancholy hanging over Jonas' head. Even though the dire situation had been all of Jonas' own making, Abraham felt his sympathies stirred up.

"I'm glad you did," said Abraham.

"Really, why?" inquired Jonas skeptically.

"Because I wanted to tell you that I forgive you."

"Seriously?"

Jonas looked unconvinced by Abraham's sudden burst of clemency and offer of redemption.

"Yeah, I do…it was pretty despicable what you did but I don't want to hold onto that hate and anger I felt. It's not healthy…for either of us. You and I won't ever be the best of friends, but I think you've suffered enough."

"Thanks, man," said Jonas gratefully, a small tear forming in the corner of his right eye.

Jonas stood up and offered Abraham his hand to shake. Abraham ignored the hand and pulled Jonas into a friendly hug. This unexpected act of amity caught the attention of more than a few of their classmates, leading to pointed looks and fervent murmurings.

"That should help with your social standing," observed Abraham good-humoredly.

"Thanks, Abe. Again, I'm so sorry."

Abraham returned back to his table where his dining companions were watching on with a combination of shock, confusion and amazement.

"You're not mad at me, are you?" Abraham tentatively asked Lincoln.

"I may not agree but I respect your choice. You're more forgiving than I am, but that's part of why I love ya, Beau." Lincoln leaned forward and gave Abraham a gentle kiss. "Let's dance."

They took to the floor and whirled about the dance floor, along with a majority of their classmates. The small, live band in the corner played a mix of modern hits with the occasional jaunty tune from the distant past thrown in to keep things interesting.

Before too long, it was time for the awards of the night. Since Jonas' disgrace it was implausible that he and Penny would be the King and Queen so the titles were definitely up for grabs, with no clear victors in sight. Mrs. Mears, dressed in a daring red number that showed off her toned physique, took to the stage with several golden envelopes, containing the names of the winners, in hand.

"Don't you all look fabulous tonight, Ladies and Gentlemen! Now, the votes have been counted it's time to announce the Royal Court."

An excited titter went through the crowd, speculation running wild as to who might take home the crowns.

"I'm pleased to announce that your Prom King is…Tobias Fletcher and your lovely Queen is…Lydia Monroe."

There was much clapping and the odd holler from the crowd, as the couple took their place center stage and courteously received their Royal headwear and sashes. Abraham applauded loudly, happy for his friend and co-captain.

The rest of the awards were given out in short order with the biggest applause going to the Court Jester, which had been predictably won by Eli, due to his hilarious mascot antics. Abraham noted that Topher was understandably beaming with pride as his boyfriend took the stage to claim his prize. The last award to be given for the evening was for 'Best-Dressed Couple'. Given how splendid everyone looked, Abraham hadn't the faintest idea of who would win. Abraham's eyes scanned over the crowd, trying to guess who it may be when he heard the most surprising thing come out of Mrs. Mears' mouth.

"Abraham Chadwick and Lincoln Shaw."

It took Abraham a few seconds to realize that he hadn't been hallucinating and that he and Lincoln had in fact won. He turned to Lincoln, who was looking at Abraham with his customary brilliant white smile. Taking Lincoln by the hand, Abraham led the way to the stage and together they graciously accepted their sashes and bowed regally before the King and Queen, before taking their places with the rest of the Royal Court. Abraham gladly accepted the applause while taking in the sea of happy faces before him. Joy flooded through his body and practically shone from his face. Turning to Lincoln, he saw the very same emotion being reflected back.

This feels too good to be true.

The rest of the evening soon whirled past in a flurry of dances and people slowly started to drift off. Some were going on to after parties, while others had rented rooms in the hotel for obvious reasons. Among the latter were Abraham and Lincoln who walked to the lobby and caught the elevator to the eleventh floor where a suite – and a promised night of passion – awaited them.

* * *

For their night of intended conjugal bliss, the lads had reserved a deluxe suite, complete with a wrap-around balcony that afforded sweeping views out over the harbor and the city. Lincoln's mother, Claire – an intelligent woman in her early forties with voluptuous curves, a coffee-colored complexion and cropped, bleach-blonde hair – worked as an executive for Babylon Enterprises, the conglomerate who owned the hotel, and was able to get the boys the suite at a much-reduced rate. She much preferred that her son and his boyfriend celebrated their night in a respectable hotel rather than in some dirty dive, for which the boys were thoroughly grateful. Abraham's parents also knew of the couple's plan to spend the night together but trusted their son's judgment.

Alone in the elevator on the way up to the room the boys couldn't keep their hands to themselves and kissed furiously, barely managing to not undress one another right then and there. Exiting the elevator far more disheveled than when they'd entered, and with the pants of their suits bulging noticeably, Abraham and Lincoln swiftly made their way to their room. Fortunately, the floor was deserted and there was no one around to witness the results of their amorous mischief.

After a quick swipe of the keycard, the passionate lads were inside the door of the suite and secured away from the world. Once the door shut behind them, they wasted no time in ardently attacking one another again. Their suits were quickly discarded to the floor as they made their way to the bedroom, via a series of increasingly intense kisses. When they reached the king-sized bed, the pair fell down together in a happy mess of limbs and quickly jettisoned the remainder of their clothing. Naked and aroused, they began to hungrily devour one another.

Earlier in the day, the boys had dropped off their overnight bags in the room, which, while containing a change of clothes to wear home the next day, also held romantic paraphernalia – candles, champagne and the like – but at present they were too overcome with passion to even look out the window at the view, let alone take the time to set the mood. Besides it would've been nigh on impossible to make them any more ready for what was to come.

The two naked forms thrashed together, their skin rapidly becoming slick with the perspiration generated by the heat of their passionate embrace. Moans and sighs filled the room, as they hurtled towards finally consummating their long held desire. Much like animals in heat, their play became even more ravenous…kissing, biting and pawing at one another's bodies. Maneuvering around onto their sides, the boys soon fastened themselves into an enthusiastic sixty-nine, eagerly devouring each other's erections.

Abraham was enjoying the foreplay immensely and feasted on Lincoln's crotch with gusto but his mind was focused on one particular burning goal. Taking a hold of Lincoln's round buttocks, Abraham used his hands to spread them apart while his fingers worked in towards the center. The digits crept their way forward until they met at the puckered entrance and started to massage around the sensitive hole, causing Lincoln to groan in response.

Obviously guessing where Abraham's desires were leading, Lincoln broke free of their embrace and lay on his back. He spread his legs wide, offering himself up to Abraham, who was in no need of further encouragement.

Diving forwards onto his stomach, Abraham gripped Lincoln's muscular thighs in each hand to keep his legs suspended in the air. Without hesitation, Abraham shoved his face roughly between the ass cheeks, forcing his tongue deep inside the musky tunnel, priming the passageway for the imminent invasion.

After gorging himself for a solid five minutes, Abraham sat back on his knees and reached for his bag by the bed. He retrieved the lubricant and squeezed a dollop of the viscous liquid into his palm. Coating his manhood thoroughly, Abraham then used the remaining lube to work his long fingers into Lincoln's wonderfully tight hole. Abraham inserted his middle finger, followed closely by his ring finger, the two digits moving in a strong circular motion, edging deeper inside with every rotation. The tips of his fingers grazed across Lincoln's prostate causing his body to jerk in pleasure. Happy with the reaction, Abraham brought them back to the special spot, massaging it and greatly enjoying the sight of Lincoln writhing in pleasure.

A near constant stream of precum oozed from the tip of Lincoln's swollen glans, leaving a clear, sticky trail across his defined abdominals. Abraham's own manhood was in a similar state of leakage, his body almost humming from excitement.

"I need ya in me, Beau" begged Lincoln, clearly desperate to be taken.

Eager to comply, Abraham removed his fingers and placed his slick cockhead at the moist entrance. Abraham began to push, adoring the feeling of the sphincter slowly opening wider to grant him access. The head suddenly popped inside the entrance, surrounding it with warmth.

I can't believe I'm actually doing this!

Lincoln flinched at first but then reached up and gripped Abraham's hips, drawing him in closer. Abraham carefully slid in, inch-by-inch, not wanting to cause his boyfriend any pain. He needn't have worried, as the only look he could see in Lincoln's eyes was one of pure, unadulterated lust. After a minute, Abraham was in all the way to hilt, with his balls resting gently against Lincoln's delectable derriere. The sensation of the hot, velvety tunnel fully encasing his manhood almost caused Abraham to explode straight away, but he was determined to stave off his orgasm for as long as possible. Abraham leaned forward and gave Lincoln a languid, loving kiss, as he leisurely started to pump into his groaning boyfriend. It felt even better than he'd imagined. As much as he wanted it to last, Abraham's baser instincts proved too hard to fight and he was soon pounding hard, much to Lincoln's delight.

"Fuck, yes, Beau!" he panted between thrusts.

Within a minute, the load that had been building in Abraham's balls could no longer be contained. His body trembled as he began to ejaculate inside Lincoln's welcoming passage. Spurt after spurt erupted from his throbbing manhood, as he gave one last thrust and held himself in tight against Lincoln. Gasping for breath, Abraham collapsed down onto Lincoln who welcomed him with open arms, the two mouths coming together into a gentle kiss.

"That was fucking awesome," murmured Abraham, in a haze of contentment.

"Ya got that right!" agreed Lincoln.

"Sorry I was so quick." Abraham's self-conscious side made a rare return appearance.

"It's fine, Beau," reassured Lincoln. "Ya lasted a heck of a lot longer than I did my first time."

"Can I help you out now?" asked Abraham, grasping Lincoln's still very erect member in his hand.

"Ready to try the other way?"

"Damn straight, Mister!" exclaimed Abraham enthusiastically. "But really, really, slow, OK?"

"Of course, Beau."

Lincoln grabbed for the bottle by the bed and thoroughly lubricated his erection and Abraham's virgin hole. To make it easier for his boyfriend, Lincoln stayed lying on his back and let Abraham straddle him, in order to be able to lower himself at his own pace onto the throbbing erection.

Abraham's desire overrode his nervousness and he sat back a tad too quickly, with the head and about half the shaft racing inside. This caused a sharp pain and a quick intake of breath on Abraham's behalf.

"Y'OK?" asked Lincoln, the concern evident in his face and voice.

"Yeah, just too greedy," said Abraham grimacing.

"Take your time, and ease into it, Beau. I ain't going nowhere."

"It's OK." Abraham's face relaxed and a small smile crept over his lips. "It feels kinda good now."

Abraham recommenced his slow descent, relishing the strange new sensation of the fat inches stretching out his no-longer-virgin tunnel. It felt natural and oh-so-right, as the former discomfort melted away into pleasure.

Eventually, he felt Lincoln's hips pressed against his buttocks. He stayed there for a few minutes just enjoying the feeling of fullness, while Lincoln's hands ran lovingly over his torso. Abraham contracted his passage around the manhood inside him, savoring the sounds of Lincoln's moans in response to the pressure. After giving himself enough time to adjust, Abraham gingerly lifted himself up and down while his boyfriend moved his hips in a circular motion beneath him. Abraham's body felt more alive than ever and he couldn't decide what he liked more – being inside Lincoln or the other way around – but he had every intention of trying many more times to find out. Each felt amazing in its own way and made him feel amazingly close to his lover.

Maybe I'm versatile?

After a little while, the pair changed positions; first with Abraham on his hands and knees and then on his back. Each time they changed it seemed that Lincoln managed to hit a previously undiscovered spot inside Abraham and send thrills of ecstasy through his body.

I can't believe I waited so long to do this!

They managed to make their way back to their original position with Abraham riding Lincoln hard, like a cock-starved cowboy. As enjoyable as it had been, Abraham was becoming slightly sore from his efforts and wanted to finish off. He started to jack himself furiously, desperate to cum while full of his boyfriend's manhood.

Taking this as a signal, Lincoln pounded upwards with an increased power, their bodies smacking loudly together. Naturally, this had the desired effect and within moments Abraham's body tensed up ahead of his second orgasm of the evening.

"I'm…I'm…"

That was all Abraham managed to get out before he started to shake and ropes of thick white cream spewed forth from his cock and splattered all over Lincoln's sweaty, heaving chest. This brought about a chain reaction, as the pressure of Abraham's ass contracting caused Lincoln to reach his much-needed release. His semen escaped its testicular confinement and sprayed inside his boyfriend, coating the velvety tunnel in gooey whiteness. Lincoln pulled Abraham down into a sweaty embrace. The couple lay together, gently kissing and smiling at one another.

"How ya doing, Beau?" inquired Lincoln softly.

"I'm a little tender but it was *so* worth it!" exclaimed Abraham. "How did I do?"

"Ya took it like a real man," joked Lincoln. "Frankly my dear, ya were born to bottom!"

"As long as it's for you, I'd do it every day!"

"Only if ya return the favor."

"It's a deal," agreed Abraham, sealing their accord with a fierce kiss.

Suddenly, Lincoln hopped up and headed out of the room. Abraham enjoyed the pleasing view of his boyfriend's naked behind walking away but was curious as to where he was headed.

"Stay here," instructed Lincoln from the doorway.

Abraham wasn't sure what his boyfriend was up to but given how satisfied he was currently feeling he had no great desire to get up and investigate. Fifteen minutes later, Lincoln returned, took Abraham by the hand and led him to the bathroom, which was aglow with the light of about fifty candles. The bubbling hot tub was frothing wildly with the entire bottle of bubble bath that Lincoln had added to it. By the side, there was a magnum of champagne – pink, of course – chilling in a bucket with two glasses on the ledge beside it.

"Time for romance," declared Lincoln, as he helped Abraham climb into the hot tub.

Together, they sank into the wonderful soapy warmth and let the water caress their strained bodies. Abraham relaxed against the side, his eyes half-closed, half-believing that it was all a dream – one he never wanted to wake up from. In the meantime, Lincoln occupied himself with opening the champagne. The familiar 'pop' of the cork brought Abraham back to the waking world and Lincoln offered him a glass filled with the delicious-looking, bubbling rose-colored liquid.

"To us!" said Lincoln, his eyes sparkling with happiness.

"To sex!" added Abraham with a cheeky grin.

The twosome chuckled together and clinked their glasses. The champagne reminded Abraham of their ill-fated Valentine's Day evening, but all those unpleasant memories soon faded away in the post-coital glow dominating his system. They sipped and cuddled, both with wide smiles on their faces. Abraham loved the look of the white bubbles splashing around his boyfriend's caramel-colored skin.

Lincoln placed his glass back on the ledge at the side of the tub and hopped onto his boyfriend's lap, facing him. The loved-up lads recommenced kissing, while Abraham's rehardened cock poked between Lincoln's buttocks in a friendly manner. Abraham moved his head down and teased Lincoln's dark brown nipples with his teeth, while his hands ran the length of his boyfriend's torso, his nails lightly scratching the skin as they went.

Abraham began to push his manhood harder up against Lincoln's entrance, eager to be inside him once again. The slickness of the soapy water soon allowed Abraham to breach his boyfriend's sphincter, although the recent fucking undoubtedly helped things along. Lincoln offered no protest as Abraham forced his way back inside, bit-by-bit, only moaning softly as he was cocked. Abraham was in far less of a rush this time and was leisurely exploring the tunnel with long sensual movements, holding Lincoln in a tight embrace.

After a little while, Lincoln took charge, supporting himself on the sides of the hot tub, as he bounced up and down, almost coming completely off the solid erection before slamming downwards and impaling himself, taking Abraham to the hilt. The water splashed violently around them, spilling onto the white tiled floor and drenching the bathmats, not that either boy was particularly concerned with anything but their frantic coupling.

This energetic fucking lasted a good fifteen minutes before a change of scene was advocated.

"Shower time?" suggested Abraham, who was keen to try as many positions and locations as possible in their short stay.

"Lead the way, Beau."

They cautiously climbed out of the tub, careful not to slip on the extremely wet and slippery floor. Once in the shower, with the rainforest showerhead pounding water down upon them, Lincoln pushed Abraham up against the blue and gold tiled wall and began to penetrate his boyfriend. With a little bit of effort, and using a good deal of conditioner as lubricant, Lincoln was soon wedged balls deep inside Abraham, lightly biting the nape of his neck, as their lust-filled sounds of pleasure echoed throughout the bathroom.

Half an hour later, their skin had become too pruned-up from all the water fun and so they returned to the bedroom to continue their play. This time Lincoln laid facedown, and did the splits, his legs spread along the edge of the bed, leaving himself wide open for Abraham who didn't need any more of an invitation. After reapplying the lube, Abraham was ready and raring to go. He squatted by the bed, lined up with Lincoln's exposed entrance and shoved his manhood roughly inside. Abraham then proceeded to jackhammer into his boyfriend, rivulets of sweat cascading down his body.

Over the course of the night, the happy couple flip-flopped several times, even taking the action onto the balcony, sodomizing each other while admiring the twinkling lights of the city. The pair only stopped their lovemaking out of sheer exhaustion. Their bodies were sore, their balls were well and truly empty but they couldn't have been happier. As the early light of dawn began to filter through their curtains, the lads drifted off into a peaceful, contented sleep.

Later that morning, Abraham woke up feeling unbelievably cheerful – and a touch tender in his nether regions. He was lying on his side with Lincoln's muscular arms wrapped around him and his buttocks nestled into his boyfriend's hips with a very erect member nestled between the crease. In some ways it felt like everything had changed. Abraham definitely felt more grown up and closer to Lincoln but he realized that the world was still spinning around as it had before. Even though he wished they'd managed to do the deed months ago, he was glad that circumstances had forced them to wait for the exact right moment.

Despite their adventures from the night before, Abraham was suddenly very keen to go again. He wriggled against the cock behind him, until the head was nudging at his, now unchaste, rosebud. His entrance was still sufficiently lubed from the night before so it didn't take much for the erection to invade him anew.

In a state of half-wakefulness, Lincoln began to nibble on Abraham's neck while steadily thrusting forward to meet his boyfriend's backward motions. Lincoln reached down and grabbed a hold of Abraham's stiff member in a firm grip and started to jack it slowly.

"Morning, Beau," he whispered.

"Wish we could wake up every morning like this."

"Me too."

Their movements increased in tempo and their amorous actions soon resulted in a series of explosions. Abraham sprayed his load into the already well-soiled sheets and Lincoln seeded his boyfriend's ass, yet again. Resting together in the afterglow of their orgasms it would have been all too easy to go back to sleep. Unfortunately, the blare of Abraham's alarm broke them out of their half-slumber, and indicated that their magical time in the room had come to its end.

Reluctantly, the pair got up and showered. They gathered their belongings and left their hotel room with a certain radiance about them, smiling like lovesick fools. Indeed, the boys practically floated down to reception on their own little cloud of happiness.

"Did you enjoy your stay?" inquired the impeccably dressed, brunette receptionist.

The lads exchanged a knowing look and Abraham struggled with the urge to gush uncontrollably about how happy he was, but managed to just smile and reply to her like a normal person.

"Yes, it was great. Thank you very much."

After settling their bill, they grabbed their overnight bags and jumped into a taxi to ferry them back home to the real world, holding hands the entire journey home.

I can't wait to do to it again!

* * *

Ever since the prom, the boys had been fornicating like crazy, every opportunity they got – in Lincoln's car, the showers at school and their bedrooms. Abraham had become far more daring and his intense cravings for his boyfriend's body overruled any worries he'd formerly had over being caught. Topher was quite correct in his assertion that once Abraham started in the ways of carnality he'd been well and truly hooked.

Following one such session, the pair were lying together naked in Abraham's bed, holding each other as their sweaty, cum-stained bodies gradually cooled after their energetic play. Abraham's parents had taken his sister to a horse fair in a neighboring city, so the lads had all day to amuse themselves in private.

Even though their relationship was going from strength to strength there was still one issue that threatened to derail their happiness. School was nearly over and the boys had been talking more and more about their futures, particularly if they were both going to be attending Port Davinica University the following semester.

For his part, Lincoln seemed to be very much leaning towards the idea of deferring his studies and going abroad for a year. He was also doing his very best to convince Abraham to do the same and explore Europe with him; an option Abraham was having some trouble contemplating. It wasn't that he didn't want to travel, he did. Rather, he wasn't sure if he was ready to spend so much time away from everything he knew and held dear – with the exception of Lincoln, of course. Abraham had given the matter a great deal of thought but was no closer to a decision.

"I could see maybe going for the summer but being away for a whole year is a bit overwhelming," admitted Abraham.

"Why?"

"Well you know I've only ever left the *state* one time...I don't know if I'm ready for such a big step. Besides, my parents would probably freak."

"Ya don't know until you ask them. My momma is fine with it."

"I don't know," said Abraham, his tone full of uncertainty.

"Look, I want ya to come, but...I think...I think I'm going to go even if ya don't."

Abraham sat up in a panic. It hadn't occurred to him that Lincoln might go without him.

Does he want to breakup?

"What will that mean for us?" asked Abraham fearfully.

Lincoln sat up as well and put his muscular arm around his boyfriend, pulling him in close to his well-developed chest.

"Well...if you're dead keen on staying then we can always do the long distance thing. I mean we can Skype and chat every day. I love ya and I wanna be with ya but this is something I need to do before going straight into more study. Can ya understand where I'm coming from?" Lincoln asked hopefully.

Abraham took a few moments to reflect on the option that Lincoln had lay before him – it wasn't particularly appealing.

Long distance would suck!

"I...I *do* understand but I...I just don't know if I can come."

"Will ya keep an open mind about it at least?"

"I guess."

Taking Abraham's face gently into his hands, Lincoln gave him a gentle kiss.

"Promise," asked Lincoln, his eyes brimming with love.

"Yes, I promise."

"Good, now I think we have other business to attend to."

Lincoln gestured down to the sheet, which was tented with his erection. Abraham wasted no time in eagerly jumping on top of his boyfriend and the two soon began passionately kissing once more – it had been a good half hour since their last copulation, after all.

Roughly an hour later, they were lying peacefully together and Abraham had his head resting on Lincoln's chest. He could hear the steady thump of his boyfriend's heart below him and it filled him with such a wonderful sense of contentment. In that moment he knew what he was going to do, he just hoped that his decision was the right one.

* * *

The last day of their senior year dawned clear and bright, rather fortunate considering that their graduation ceremony was being held outside on the lawn of St. Francis Xavier's lush, botanical garden. The students looked resplendent in their black cap and gowns, sparking many a tear and many a photo. The ceremony itself was a formal affair, with a few notable alumni – including a State senator, a Pulitzer Prize winning journalist and the current Mayor of Port Davinica – in attendance to farewell the graduating class. Mercifully, their speeches had been short, yet poignant, so the students and guests didn't become too restless.

That evening, Abraham and Lincoln were standing with their families in the Chadwicks' living room to celebrate the joyous occasion. Abraham's parents had courteously invited Lincoln's mother, Claire, and his Aunt Gloria to join them.

After Abraham had posed for yet another series of photos, for his camera-happy parents, his father handed him a plain white envelope.

"What's this?" asked Abraham, more than a little puzzled.

"We were going to get you a car, Nemo, but we decided that you might enjoy this just a little bit more," said Burt mysteriously.

Abraham opened the envelope and saw that it was a check for ten thousand dollars.

"But, what…"

"It should be enough to last you a good while you're in Europe together," said Abraham's mother, her voice wobbling with the start of tears.

Abraham hadn't yet told them of his choice to take a year off and travel with Lincoln but they seemed to be already way ahead of him. He'd been hesitant to broach the subject, as he feared they might try and talk him out of his decision.

On Lincoln's side, his mother had been nothing but supportive and had even given Lincoln a generously charged-up debit card to see him through his year abroad. He also planned to sell his jeep to Austin to help fund their foreign escapades.

"Oh my god, thank you guys!" exclaimed Abraham, hugging them both. "But how did you know?"

"You may think we're old but we're not deaf. We've heard you talking about it with Lincoln for the last few weeks," teased Burt. "And then we had a little chat with Claire."

"Momma? Why didn't you tell us that you told them?" demanded Lincoln.

"You never asked," laughed Claire.

"You two aren't the only ones who can keep a secret," added Sheila, with a certain malicious glee.

"And you guys are really OK with it all?" asked Abraham a little unbelievingly.

"Of course, we just want you to be happy, Nemo. But we also want you to come back and not feel like you've missed out on anything," replied Burt.

"You're so lucky! Although I want a car when I graduate," remarked Megan.

"We'll see young lady," replied Sheila, clearly not wanting to have that discussion just yet.

Abraham couldn't believe that his parents had been so generous, or so at ease with his decision. Admittedly, he shouldn't have been too surprised since both his father and mother had traveled a great deal before they'd decided to settle down and have a family.

"Time for a toast," called Burt, retrieving the champagne from the kitchen and filling the glasses. "To our wonderful sons and their next adventures!"

Everyone raised their glasses and partook of the bubbly liquid. Even Megan was allowed a little sip although she soon declared her disgust.

"This is awful. Why would anyone want to drink it?"

This elicited a round of laughter from the group, causing Megan to scowl slightly.

"Time for more photos," declared Abraham's father.

The boys dutifully posed for seemingly hundreds more photos with their diplomas, although Abraham thought that the inordinate amount that they'd taken at the ceremony had been more than sufficient. However, given his parents' recent generosity he wasn't about to complain…within their earshot, at any rate.

Eventually, they were released from their familial duties and were free to get changed out of their gowns and into more appropriate attire to go celebrate with the rest of their classmates. The main graduation party was being held at Eli's – his huge pool and parents' well stocked bar were the main draw cards – and promised to be a very raucous affair. By the time the boys got there it was in full swing with many a former-high schooler in good spirits – not to mention full of them. Abraham was exceedingly careful in keeping an eye on his drinks, as was Lincoln, neither wishing a repeat of the victory party. The duo partied until well into the night until they finally crashed out in Eli's bed – right next to Topher and Eli. It wasn't too crowded as the over-sized bed could have easily slept six…and had already, if rumor was to be believed about Eli's pre-Topher antics.

Abraham awoke the next morning with a fuzzy head and vague memories of a spectacular party. He turned his head to look at his slumbering bedmates and smiled, before closing his eyes and attempting to sleep off the rest of his hangover.

* * *

One month had passed since their graduation and once again Abraham and Lincoln were surrounded by their nearest and dearest, but this time the mood was tinged by an underlying sorrow. They were sitting in a big group in the café nearest the doors for international departures of the bustling Lucien James Airport, at the northern outskirts of Port Davinica. While there was much talking and excitement, there were more than a few glistening eyes that betrayed the sadness beneath.

Looking around, Abraham could see that there were a few other highly emotional groupings about the place, obviously in similar situations of impending separation. The café echoed with a babble of conversation, as everyone seemed to want the last word.

"You can always come home. We'll be waiting."

"Just call if you need anything."

"Don't forget to Skype."

"Oh, I wish I was going instead."

There was laughter and tears and much promising to stay in regular contact. They had arrived a few hours in advance, as their parents had been concerned about not making the flight.

Abraham had been ready and raring to go from 6am that morning. There had also been a last minute frantic search for his passport, which was found behind the couch in the lounge room. It seems that a mischievous Captain Reynolds had hidden it when Abraham was in the bathroom – it was almost like he didn't want Abraham to go. He and his faithful companion had also had a very tearful goodbye that morning.

"Look after Cap for me?" Abraham had asked his sister.

"Of course, I will," agreed Megan. "As long as you bring me back all sorts of cool stuff."

"Deal."

They hugged and Megan burst into a flood of tears. Abraham was touched and knew he'd miss his little sister more than he'd like to admit.

The boys had had a farewell party at Lincoln's house the previous weekend to say a proper goodbye to their friends, which had likewise been full of mixed emotions. Even so, a small contingent – Topher, Eli, Tobias, Lydia, Austin and Cassidy – had insisted on showing up at the airport to bid a heartfelt farewell to the departing duo.

"Now you two better behave yourselves while we're gone," Abraham had teased Topher.

"Only if you promise to misbehave," countered Topher smirking, although his eyes betrayed his despondency.

"I'll see what I can do."

The group stayed together in the café and drew the process out as long as they could but all too soon it was time to go through the gates and pass the security checks in order to begin their brand new journey together. When they reached the entrance to the international departures the tears started flowing freely, with nary a dry eye left amongst the group. Abraham's face was wet from weeping, as he hugged his friends and then his parents goodbye.

As sad as Abraham was to be leaving everyone behind he was also bursting with excitement for the year ahead and what exciting exploits awaited him and Lincoln across the ocean. Abraham turned to Lincoln and gave him a broad smile.

"Ready?"

"Always, Beau."

Abraham look Lincoln's hand and together they waved goodbye to the assembled crowd until the last possible second, then walked through the gates and on towards their next adventure.

* * *

Just over one year later, summer was once more drawing to a close. Abraham was in bed, lying on his side, naked, and lightly tracing the outline of Lincoln's recent tattoo. By itself it looked like a simplistic drawing of a bird but when paired with the complimentary one on Abraham's torso it formed a heart when they embraced, which was often. The new additions had healed nicely with the last of the redness fading a few days prior.

They were currently staying in Barcelona, the latest in a long line of cities, and one of Abraham's favorites so far. The afternoon sun filled the room with heat and light, and the curtains by the entrance to the terrace rose and fell gently with the soft breeze off of the sea. The sounds of street life drifted up from below –

snippets of conversation, the clatter of heels on the sidewalk and the occasional car horn. The smells from the Tapas restaurant at the base of their building were also carried up on the gentle wind giving them the occasional tantalizing waft of deliciously fried food. The room also held the scent of their recent play, which had dried on the thin sheets and their skin. Their ardor and need for one another hadn't been diminished by their time spent together, if anything it had increased – they were healthy, virile young men, after all.

The couple had been on quite the journey since leaving Port Davinica, but part of Abraham was glad that they would soon be heading home to their families and to resume their studies. The boys had soaked up a good deal of what Europe had to offer in the past year and gone through an alarming amount of money in the process. Fortunately, they'd been able to supplement their savings through working in bars and cafes, and even gogo dancing at one point – the tips and free drinks had been well worth it.

Both lads had become much more worldly and experienced after having sown their wild oats, spreading their seed far and wide. With Lincoln by his side, Abraham continued to blossom. Long gone was that timid, clean-cut boy who kept to the edges, shying away from the center of things. He'd even changed physically as well as emotionally. Abraham had let his hair grow and it was now nearly down to his shoulders and had become an even more vibrant shade of red due to the Spanish sun. Lincoln had also grown out his hair with a magnificently fluffy Afro now adorning the top of his head.

It had continued to be a year of firsts for Abraham, from those special cookies in Amsterdam, to marching in Pride parades all around the Continent…and that mind-blowing, decadent orgy in Berlin. Indeed, Abraham had become quite the capable cocksman in his time away, knowing well how to please his man…and others. While Abraham was glad for the other experience, it had made him even surer of Lincoln. He was much more confident in himself and his relationship, and he now carried a mature attitude that belied his twenty years. At times it seemed as if Lincoln had to run to keep up with his newly adventurous boyfriend.

"I've created a monster!" Lincoln often proclaimed jokingly.

"Yeah, but I'm your monster."

The whole trip had been like a honeymoon of sorts. Of course, they'd had their little spats along the way but nothing that hadn't been able to be fixed by a vigorous helping of makeup sex.

Beside Abraham, Lincoln stirred and looked up at him with sleepy eyes.

"What ya doing?" mumbled Lincoln, barely awake.

"Nothing," replied Abraham, his hand now tracing along the enticing curves of Lincoln's posterior. "Yet."

Abraham moved his head forward and planted a soft, tender kiss on his boyfriend's lips. The kiss quickly increased in intensity as their bodies came together, slowly grinding and rubbing against one another. Abraham moved his hand down between their writing bodies and his experienced fingers knew just what to do, expertly fondling Lincoln's cock and balls before working his way between the muscular legs to invade the ever-welcoming passageway behind.

Lincoln gasped as a digit breached his sphincter and began to explore inside, followed quite closely by a second. To grant

Abraham easier access, Lincoln moved onto his back, opening his legs wide.

Moving downwards, Abraham stopped to tease Lincoln's dark-brown, dime-sized nipples with his tongue and teeth, causing them to become erect nubs. He then hungrily nuzzled Lincoln's fragrant armpits before he worked his way down the writhing body, licking the smooth mocha-colored skin that tasted just as good as it looked.

Abraham reached Lincoln's erect manhood, which was glistening with a copious amount of precum. Taking his time, Abraham tongued all round the manhood, licking along the creases between the solid legs and Lincoln's tasty, masculine-scented groin. When he reached the smooth, heavy ball sack, Abraham took it into his mouth and began to roll it around with a practiced ease.

Eventually, he made his way back up to the tip of Lincoln's manhood, licking the head clean before taking the cock down his throat in a big gulp making Lincoln cry out in pleasure. He worked the shaft with his hand and mouth and after only a few minutes, Abraham could feel his boyfriend's body tense up as he got close to the edge. He backed off, softly kissing and licking the shaft before beginning the assault anew. Abraham did this several times, bringing his lover right to the brink and whisking him away from it again. He loved edging Lincoln, and himself for that matter, as it always made the ejaculation even more intense when it was finally released.

When he was done torturing Lincoln in this marvelous manner, Abraham lifted his mouth off of the thoroughly delicious cock and grabbed a hold of Lincoln's hips. He lifted them up, bringing Lincoln's exposed hole closer to his face, before shoving his face right into the crevice, his tongue burrowing deep inside. He inhaled deeply, savoring the familiar musky scent. Then in a forceful move, Abraham flipped Lincoln over and pulled him over the edge of the bed. He spat into his hand for extra lubrication, although Lincoln was still moist from their earlier encounter, and then forced his weapon inside. The passageway clamped down on his cock in a powerful grip, massaging his manhood with its velvety embrace.

Abraham leaned forward, his torso pressing against Lincoln's muscular back, and began to lick and tenderly bite the nape of his boyfriend's neck. He then started to move his hips in small, measured movements, slowly letting Lincoln adjust to the manhood probing inside him.

It wasn't long before Abraham increased his tempo, hitting slightly deeper inside with each thrust. The constant movement stimulated Lincoln's pleasure spot, causing him to grip the sheet tightly and strain against the bed, his muscles taut and glistening. Their grunts of passion echoed out over the rooftops but seeing that their building was quite popular with gentleman of a certain persuasion, such sounds were not an uncommon occurrence. Abraham grabbed Lincoln by this thick hair and pulled back as he continued to mercilessly hammer away into the bubble butt.

This was about as much stimulation as Lincoln could bear and his cock suddenly pulsed, releasing his pent-up load onto their already cum-soaked sheets. Not wanting to be left behind, Abraham quickly pulled out and within a handful of hasty strokes shot his seed all over the round globes of Lincoln's muscular buttocks. The sticky, white cream gradually dripped its way downward, running down the sides of his hips and legs.

It was a sight Abraham had seen quite a few times before and was one he could never imagine tiring of.

So fucking hot!

Abraham collapsed down on top of Lincoln, as their ragged breathing slowed down, falling in sync to a more regular pace. Together, they lay there, sated and outrageously head over heels in love.

"Pity we can't stay like this forever," whispered Abraham.

"Gotta get back to the real world some time, Beau."

"I know."

Lincoln flipped over, throwing Abraham on his back, and then jumped on top of his boyfriend, pinning him to the bed. Abraham adored the pressure of his boyfriend's well-developed frame bearing down on him.

"And even when we're back in Port Davinica, I'm still gonna jump on ya any chance I get!" promised Lincoln, his eyes aflame with lust.

Abraham looked down and saw that Lincoln was at full mast once again.

"Best we keep in practice then," agreed Abraham, his own member stirring into action.

"As you wish, Beau."

Abraham pulled Lincoln back down to him and the two became happily lip-locked as their bodies came fully together to make love.

Damn, I love this man!

ABOUT THE AUTHOR

Jimi could be considered to be something of a refined blend of Australian/Polish heritage – given his passion for the arts, vodka and BBQs. He now lives in Paris with his wonderfully understanding French husband and cats.

For other of his raunchy ramblings and published work, feel free to browse http://www.jimify.me follow him on Twitter & Instagram @jimifyme or show your devotion at facebook.com/JIMIFY.ME

IN PRINT FROM LYDIAN PRESS

DOM'S DELIGHTS

Come on in and taste the love!

Dom has worked hard pursuing his dreams of delighting the masses with his tasty treats - indeed his cream has been eagerly eaten all about the town. Now he has almost everything he ever dreamed of – a successful business, loving friends and a beautiful beau. There's just one more thing he needs to make his life complete...to finally marry the man of his dreams!

BEST SERVED HOT

Revenge has never been sweeter.

When Jameson loses everything he holds dear, he almost drowns in a sea of despair. Bitter and broken, he shuns his friends and retreats from the world. Then a chance encounter with a handsome young man offers him a glimmer of hope, and he slowly begins to piece his life back together. Will he be given the second chance at the love he so desperately deserves?

A MAN FOR EVERY OCCASION

There's always time for love.

The bustling city of Port Davinica is home to many stories of love, lust and more than a few happy endings. Follow the adventures of these men as they find love in all manner of places with an amorous touch of the supernatural thrown in for good measure. You'll soon discover in this collection of romantic tales that no matter the festive occasion – Halloween, Christmas, and especially Valentine's Day - there's always time for love.

Lydian Press is dedicated to bringing you the finest
GLBTQ erotic literature on the web.

Visit us on the web at:

http://lydianpress.com